NASHVILLE – BOOK TWO –
HAMMER AND A SONG

NASHVILLE – BOOK TWO – HAMMER AND A SONG

INGLATH COOPER

Contents

Copyright

Books by Inglath Cooper

My Italian Lover – What If – Book One
Fences
Dragonfly Summer – Book Two – Smith Mountain Lake
Series
Blue Wide Sky – Book One – Smith Mountain Lake Series
That Month in Tuscany
Crossing Tinker's Knob
Jane Austen Girl
Good Guys Love Dogs
Truths and Roses
Nashville – Part Ten – Not Without You
Nashville – Book Nine – You, Me and a Palm Tree
Nashville – Book Eight – R U Serious
Nashville – Book Seven – Commit
Nashville – Book Six – Sweet Tea and Me
Nashville – Book Five – Amazed
Nashville – Book Four – Pleasure in the Rain
Nashville – Book Three – What We Feel
Nashville – Book Two – Hammer and a Song
Nashville – Book One – Ready to Reach
On Angel's Wings
A Gift of Grace
RITA® Award Winner John Riley's Girl
A Woman With Secrets
Unfinished Business
A Woman Like Annie
The Lost Daughter of Pigeon Hollow
A Year and a Day

Reviews

Readers who have enjoyed the emotional stories of authors like Colleen Hoover may enjoy this live-your-dream story where "Inglath Cooper draws you in with her words and her amazing characters. It is a joy to pick up these books. There is just the right amount of love and romance with the perfect dose of reality. The dialogue is relatable and you just fall in love with the story."

♪

"Truths and Roses . . . so sweet and adorable, I didn't want to stop reading it. I could have put it down and picked it up again in the morning, but I didn't want to." – **Kirkusreviews.com**

On Truths and Roses: "I adored this book...what romance should be, entwined with real feelings, real life and roses blooming. Hats off to the author, best book I have read in a while." – **Rachel Dove, Frustrated Yukky Mommy Blog**

"I am a sucker for sweet love stories! This is definitely one of those! It was a very easy, well written, book. It was easy to follow, detailed, and didn't leave me hanging without answers." – **www.layfieldbaby.blogspot.com**

"I don't give it often, but I am giving it here – the sacred 10. Why? Inglath Cooper's A GIFT OF GRACE mesmerized me; I consumed it in one sitting. When I turned the last page, it was three in the morning." – **MaryGrace Meloche, Contemporary Romance Writers**

5 Blue Ribbon Rating! ". . .More a work of art than a story. . .Tragedies affect entire families as well as close loved ones, and this story portrays that beautifully as well as giving the reader hope that somewhere out there is A GIFT OF GRACE for all of us." — **Chrissy Dionne, Romance Junkies 5 Stars**

"A warm contemporary family drama, starring likable people

coping with tragedy and triumph." 4 1/2 Stars. — **Harriet Klausner**

"A GIFT OF GRACE is a beautiful, intense, and superbly written novel about grief and letting go, second chances and coming alive again after devastating adversity. Warning!! A GIFT OF GRACE is a three-hanky read…better make that a BIG box of tissues read! Wowsers, I haven't cried so much while reading a book in a long long time…Ms. Cooper's skill makes A GIFT OF GRACE totally believable, totally absorbing…and makes Laney Tucker vibrantly alive. This book will get into your heart and it will NOT let go. A GIFT OF GRACE is simply stunning in every way—brava, Ms. Cooper! Highly, highly recommended!" – **4 1/2 Hearts — Romance Readers Connection**

"…A WOMAN WITH SECRETS…a powerful love story laced with treachery, deceit and old wounds that will not heal…enchanting tale…weaved with passion, humor, broken hearts and a commanding love that will have your heart soaring and cheering for a happily-ever-after love. Kate is strong-willed, passionate and suffers a bruised heart. Cole is sexy, stubborn and also suffers a bruised heart…gripping plot. I look forward to reading more of Ms. Cooper's work!" – **www.freshfiction.com**

＊

For all the songwriters whose songs have provided the soundtrack to my life.

CeCe

I'm sitting in the middle of the truck seat with my head on Holden's shoulder when the sun begins to peep up over the Davidson County Pound building. I'm not the least bit sleepy. I'm as wide-awake as I've ever been.

Holden's hand is on my knee, his thumb rubbing back and forth over the fabric of my jeans. We haven't said anything for a good while, instead letting the music from the radio take up the space between us.

There are so many things I want to say, but I know I shouldn't. Like how is it possible to feel this kind of connection to someone you've known for such a short time? Or how I can't imagine sitting here all night, waiting to find out if Hank Junior is okay, without Holden next to me.

I know it hardly makes any sense, but it's true.

An engine sounds behind us, and I look back to see a white truck pull up. A man in a tan work uniform gets out, repositions the ball cap on his head and walks up.

Holden opens the door and steps from the truck. "Mornin'," he says to the man.

"Help you?"

"I hope so," Holden says. "Our dog is missing, and we were told an animal control officer picked him up last night. We think he might be here."

My heart does a somersault at Holden's description of Hank Junior as *our* dog. Had I really called him Grouchy Guy the first day we met?

"I'm afraid you'll have to wait until the main office opens at eight to find out."

"Are you headed down there now, sir?"

"Yeah, but I can't release him for you."

1

"Could we just go with you and make sure he's there?"

"I'm real sorry."

Tears well up from my chest and splash down my face before I even realize I'm crying. I jump out of the truck and stumble on a rock, righting myself with a hand on Holden's arm. "I'm CeCe," I say, sticking out my hand. "This is Holden."

We shake, and he points to the nametag on his shirt. "Kenny."

"Hey, Kenny. I'm kind of having a hard time with this. Hank was in a pound when he was a puppy. His first family left him at one, and he just sat in a corner of his kennel and shook. He wouldn't eat, and he–" I break off there, unable to speak past the knot in my throat. "Please. I need to know he's okay."

The man shakes his head. "It's against the rules."

My heart drops south, and I search for the words to make him understand. "He's my best friend," I say. "He needs me."

He looks at me for an endless string of moments. "I wish some of the folks who throw their dogs away here thought of them like that instead. If I get fired, maybe you can help me find a new job."

"I don't want you to lose your job, but I just want my dog back."

"Probably wouldn't be the worst thing that ever happened to me."

"Thank you so much," I say, the words pouring out in a gush of gratitude. "Thank you."

"Well, all right then." He pulls a set of keys from his pocket, walks over and opens the padlock on the gate, swinging each arm wide. "Y'all follow me."

I scramble into the truck, and Holden slides in behind me.

Neither of us says a word all the way to the building. I feel frozen to the seat, my heart pounding so hard in my chest that I know Holden must hear it.

Kenny pulls up to a side door, and we roll to a stop behind him. I hear the dogs from inside, a few barks starting up, and then more follow. By the time he steps in and flips on a light, all the dogs are awake and starting to bark.

"All right, now," Kenny says in a kind voice. "Y'all settle down."

His voice has an amazing calming effect. The barking subsides to a few rumbles of concern.

I scan the kennels in front of us, trying not to look at the faces. Already, my heart feels like it's swelled to the size of a pumpkin, and I'm afraid the sob sitting at the back of my throat is going to burst out at any second.

"Walk on down, and see if you see him," Kenny says.

I start down the aisle with Holden right behind me. I can tell he's trying to keep his gaze focused straight ahead. Halfway down, I spot Hank Junior curled up in the back of his kennel, shaking from the tip of his nose to the tip of his tail. Snuggled up next to him with its head on Hank's side is a chubby little Beagle.

"Hank," I say, my voice cracking.

He looks up, thumps his tail once as if he's afraid to believe it's really me.

Kenny steps in and says, "That him?"

"Yes," I say.

Kenny opens the door. I nearly leap inside, dropping to my knees and hugging Hank so hard he yelps. He licks my cheek though, still shaking.

"I'm sorry," I say, kissing his velvety ear, unable to hold back my tears.

Something nudges at my elbow, and I glance down to see the chubby Beagle looking up at me as if hoping to be included in the reunion.

Holden walks into the kennel and squats down beside us. He reaches out and strokes Hank's head, then does the same for the Beagle.

She all but melts under his touch and rolls over on her back. He smiles and scratches her belly.

"What's her name?" Holden asks, looking up at Kenny.

"Patsy," he says.

"As in Kline," I say, and we both smile.

Patsy turns her head and licks the back of Holden's hand. I see *him* melt a little.

"I hate to rush y'all," Kenny says, "but I've got to get to work."

I stand up and turn to face him. "Please let me take him now, Kenny. I can't leave him here. I just can't."

He looks at Hank and then back at me again. "So what kind of work did you say you have lined up for me?" he asks with a half-grin.

Before I can answer, he hands me a nylon leash and says, "Bring him on out."

I can't help it. I throw my arms around his neck and hug him hard. "Thank you. Thank you so much."

I slip the lead around Hank's neck, and he glues himself to my leg. Holden is still rubbing the Beagle. He stands reluctantly, following me through the door.

Kenny closes it and clicks the latch back in place. Patsy looks at Hank Junior, then up at us, her brown eyes suddenly sad, as if she knows she's being left. Clearly, not for the first time.

Holden points at the orange card with her name on the kennel door. "What does that mean?"

"Today is her day since nobody came for her," Kenny says, his voice flat now, as if he's had to practice saying these things without emotion.

"You mean she'll be put to sleep?" Holden asks, disbelieving.

"Yeah," Kenny says.

Holden's face goes white as chalk. I know in my heart how hard it must be for him to come in here in the first place and all the bad memories it must bring back. I kneel down and stick my hand back through the door to rub Patsy's head, feeling sick all the way down to the bottom of my stomach.

I don't see any orange cards on the other doors. I open my

mouth to ask what her adoption fee is when Holden says, "Can I adopt her?"

Kenny glances at his watch. "The front desk people won't be here until eight. The euth tech usually comes in at seven-thirty."

Holden actually looks like he might pass out. I feel sick myself, but I put a hand on his arm, maybe to steady us both.

But his voice is strong when he says, "I don't care what the fee is. I'll put it on my credit card. Let us go on and take her. I promise I'll give her a good life."

Kenny glances at Patsy, then back at Holden, and hands him another nylon lead. "Y'all come on, so I can at least fill out the paperwork."

We follow him to the front office where he opens a drawer and pulls out two forms, one for me and one for Holden. I fill out the paperwork for Hank's release, waiting while Holden finishes the application for Patsy.

"The adoption fee is fifty dollars," Kenny says.

Holden opens his wallet and counts out the cash. I notice he has one dollar left.

Kenny takes it and says, "All right, then."

"Thank you, Kenny." Holden shakes his hand.

"For her sake, I'm glad y'all were here," Kenny says, walking around the desk and reaching down to rub Patsy's head. She looks up at him and wags her tail as if to say thank you.

"I'm happy for you, girl," he says, a rasp to his voice.

"Thank you so much, Kenny," I say and give him another hug.

He nods and walks us to the door. We step outside into the crisp morning air, Hank Junior and I climbing into the truck from the passenger side, and Holden picking Patsy up and putting her in from his side.

He backs the truck out of the spot, throws a wave at Kenny, then looks over at me and smiles. A really happy smile. I smile back, and as we roar off down the drive, it feels as if we've just done something as miraculous as cheating death. Which I guess we actually have.

♪

Holden

She's got her head on my thigh. How the heck is a guy supposed to resist that?

I stroke her back with my right hand, and if the snoring is any indication, it's not long before she appears to be fast asleep.

"She knows," CeCe says, studying me from the other side of the truck.

"What?" I ask.

"That you saved her life."

"How do you know?"

"They just do. Hank Junior was the same way the day I got him out of the pound."

"I can't even imagine that someone could leave her in a place like that."

"Me, either. Thank you for getting her."

"If I hadn't, you would have."

She smiles at me, and it feels good to know we have this in common.

"Not sure what Thomas is gonna say about our new roommate."

"He's a softie like you."

"Oh, you think I'm a softie now, do you?"

"Yeah," she says with a smile that reaches her eyes. "I do."

I don't know that anyone has ever looked at me the way CeCe is looking at me now. I just know it feels good to have her approval. At the same time, I realize I probably shouldn't let myself dwell on that. That there's trouble down that road if I do.

"They might need to go to the bathroom," CeCe says.

"Yeah," I say and pull over at the next turn. We get the dogs out and walk them to a grassy spot where they both immediately do their business. We let them sniff for a couple of minutes and then get back in the truck.

A mile or so down the road, we pass a little country store with its lights on. I slam on the brakes. "Coffee?"

"Oh, my gosh, yes," she says.

I throw the truck in reverse and then swing into the parking lot. "Y'all wait here," I tell the dogs. They both wag their tails and stretch out on the seat as if they plan to get some shut-eye while we're gone.

The store is everything you would think a country store might be. The smell of homemade biscuits and coffee greets us at the door. Three older men in bib overalls sit on a wooden church pew across from the coffee pots, sipping from their cups and talking like they've got the world's problems to figure out by noon.

CeCe and I both choose a large, mine black, hers with cream. I find myself noting the choice for future reference and at the same time wonder what I'm doing.

A large lady with heavily teased hair greets us at the cash register. "Y'all out mighty early," she says, smiling like she's happy to see us.

"Rescue mission," CeCe says.

"Ah," she says, winking at me. "Fun stuff."

CeCe looks like she's going to add something, then thinks better of it. She insists on paying for the coffee. "You might need that last dollar for Patsy food," she teases.

"Hope the tips are good tonight," I say.

"Y'all enjoy your morning," the cashier calls out as we head back through the door.

Patsy and Hank Junior barely glance up as we climb in the truck. "They look like they could sleep for days," I say.

"Who could blame them?"

We drive for a few minutes, silent while we sip our coffee. With CeCe, there's no feeling of having to fill the silence with small talk. I have to admit I like that. It's not something I've experienced with anyone other than Thomas.

We round a curve, and the view opens up with a valley sloping down to our right.

"Let's pull over for a minute," CeCe suggests.

I turn the truck onto the gravel edge that looks as if it's been put there for people to stop and enjoy the view.

"That's just crazy beautiful," she says, opening her door and sliding out.

I follow her to the front of the truck. She climbs onto the hood and looks out at the valley below us. I step up and sit next to her. "Yeah, it is," I say.

The trees have that new leaf green that I imagine artists must yearn to get exactly accurate. A big red barn sits out to the right, and I can see horses grazing behind the white board fencing surrounding it.

"So are you," I say, the words slipping out before I can edit them.

CeCe looks at me, her eyes questioning.

"Crazy beautiful," I add.

She looks down, and I can see the color come into her cheeks. When she looks up at me, I reach out and touch her face with the back of my hand. I hear her short intake of breath, and it matches the electricity that zips through me from the softness of her skin.

We study each other for what feels like a good while, and without censoring what I'm feeling, I lean in and kiss her. It starts out light and testing, but then just as quickly ignites into something completely different. I snag her waist with one arm and reel her in to me. She opens her mouth beneath mine, and we kiss like we've both been waiting for it all our lives.

If so, it was worth every moment of the wait. If for nothing else, then to hear the raspy way she says my name now.

She slides her arms around my neck, and I haul her in closer, slipping my hands up the back of her shirt and under the lacy bra beneath. Her skin is like silk, and I have never wanted to touch anyone the way I want to touch her now.

I feel myself losing control and start to pull back, but CeCe presses her hands to the back of my head and deepens the kiss. We're both breathing like we just ran here from downtown Nashville, and I know if we don't stop now, there won't be any stopping at all.

I untangle myself and lie back on the truck hood, staring up at the morning blue sky and breathing hard.

"I'm sorry," CeCe says, lying down beside me, her voice regretful.

"I'm not," I say.

"You're not?"

"How could anyone be sorry about a kiss like that?"

She lets out a breath of what sounds like relief. "I thought I might have–"

"You didn't," I say. I sit up then and pull her up beside me.

"You're not the kind of girl a guy should take advantage of, CeCe."

The look on her face makes me smile.

"Yeah, right now, I kind of wish you were, too," I say.

"You'd never take advantage of anyone," she says. "But then I don't imagine you'd have to."

"Thanks, I think," I say, grinning.

She smiles at me then, and there's no denying the spool of feeling unraveling between us.

We study the view for a few moments before I say, "CeCe?"

"Yeah?"

"I don't make a habit of leading a girl on when I'm seeing someone else."

"Are you leading me on?"

"I don't really know what I'm doing."

"It's okay. Neither do I."

"Is there someone in your life?"

She shakes her head. "No one serious."

"Has there been?"

"Sort of."

"Which means?"

"Not serious enough for me to stay in Virginia."

I put my hand on the back of hers and lace our fingers together. "What do you really want out of this town, CeCe?"

She considers the question and then looks at me. "Just a chance to do what I love to do. You?"

"The same."

"You think anybody ever comes here just because they want to be famous?"

I laugh a short laugh. "Ah, yeah."

"That I don't get," she says.

"What is fame, anyway? People knowing who you are, seeing your face on the cover of some rag tabloid with whatever skeleton you happen to have in your closet peeking out?"

CeCe laughs. "Success, I get. That just means you get to do what you love because you've found a following of people who love the same thing."

"Which is not that easy, apparently."

"No one ever said it would be easy."

"But we're here, anyway."

"Yeah. We're here."

She's looking at me again with that look in her eyes, and I feel something low inside of me shift, like I might have crossed a line I'm going to have a whole lot of trouble stepping back from. I rub my thumb across the back of her hand, and then let go.

She slides off the hood and jumps to the ground. I follow, glancing over my shoulder. Hank Junior and Patsy are sitting in the middle of the seat, her head resting against his shoulder. "They look like a couple," I say.

CeCe smiles. "Yeah, they do."

"We better get them home."

She nods, and I like knowing that word includes all of us. Home.

♪

CeCe

It's almost eight a.m. by the time we park the truck in the back lot of the apartment complex. We get out and let Hank Junior and Patsy have a few minutes in the grass before we head up the stairs.

I'm so tired I feel like I can barely stand and at the same time so wired with feeling that I hardly know what to do with it. Has it really been less than eight hours since we left here last night looking for Hank? It seems like a lifetime has taken place since then.

Hank and I follow Holden and Patsy up the stairs, and I can't help but stare at his wide shoulders. My lips tingle with the memory of his kiss, and I have to stop myself from reaching for his shirt tail and pulling him to me.

At the apartment door, he sticks the key in the lock, then turns to me. "Weird as this sounds," he says, "it was kind of great being with you last night."

"Yeah," I say, "you, too."

He leans in, and I start to close my eyes in anticipation of his kiss. Just then, the door jerks open, and we both jump back from one another.

"Hey, you two," Thomas says in a tight voice I don't recognize. "Been wondering when you were gonna get back."

From behind him, a girl steps out, the look on her face clearly one of confusion. "Surprise," she says, only the word is flat, like a balloon someone has just let all the air out of.

"Sarah," Holden says, sounding as stunned as he looks.

"She drove all night to get here," Thomas says. "Isn't that something?"

"Is everything all right?" Holden asks.

Sarah glances from Holden to me, and her blue, very blue, eyes start to well with tears. "I thought it was," she says.

13

"You got a dog," Thomas throws out, as if looking for a diversion.

"Yeah," Holden says. "Her name's Patsy."

"A dog," Sarah says. "Wow. I didn't know you were–"

"It was kind of spur of the moment," he explains.

We all stand there for a few seconds like frozen popsicles, none of us sure what to do or say next. Holden moves first, stepping in to the apartment to put his arms around Sarah and hug her.

I watch, unable to move. Hank Junior whines and looks up at me, as if asking what this means. I don't dare look at him, sure I'll burst into tears if I do.

Holden steps back from the hug and waves a hand at me. "Sarah, this is CeCe. CeCe, Sarah."

We look at each other and smile, and I feel sure mine is as wobbly as hers. "Nice to meet you," we both say at the same time.

"So," Thomas says, "what a night, huh?"

"Yeah," Holden agrees, running a hand across the back of his hair.

"I bet Sarah would like to hear all about it," Thomas says. "Why don't y'all take the bedroom for some privacy, and I'll get the lowdown from CeCe out here?"

Holden looks at me, and I immediately glance away since I have no idea what to do with any of this. I feel as if a wrecking ball just landed in the center of my stomach.

"Ah, okay," Holden says. "Anything you need me to get out of your car, Sarah?"

She shakes her head. "Thomas already brought it in for me."

"You mind feeding Patsy when you feed Hank?" Holden directs the question to me.

"Sure," I say, super cheerful. "No problem."

Holden nods and walks down the hall to the bedroom. Sarah follows him. I stand perfectly still until I hear the click of the lock.

Only then do I unhook Hank's leash and let out all the air in my chest.

"I'm real sorry, CeCe," Thomas says.

"You don't need to be," I say, assuming he's talking about Hank Junior, but suspecting the apology encompasses Sarah's arrival as well. "It all worked out."

"Tell me about it?" he asks, heading for the kitchen where he pulls two bowls from the cabinet and gets the dog food out of the pantry.

While Hank Junior and Patsy scarf up their food, I lay out everything that happened at the pound, including Holden's adopting Patsy at the last minute.

"I'm glad," Thomas says. "She's a cute little thing."

"I think she and Hank are in love."

Thomas smiles and then looks at me, the smile fading, "That got a little awkward out there."

I start to act like I don't know what he's talking about and then just as quickly realize how unbelievable I would be. "Yeah," I say.

"He really didn't know she was coming," Thomas says.

"Apparently."

He leans against the sink and folds his arms across his chest. "Holden is a lot of things, but he's never been a player. I think you kind of caught him off guard."

"Timing has never really been my thing."

"They've been together almost two years. I don't want to see you hurt, CeCe."

"She's beautiful," I say. "Really beautiful."

"So are you," Thomas says.

I start to shake my head, but he adds, "You are. It's just gonna be that timing thing."

I feel the tears start to well up, try my best to stop them, but they roll down my face like a faucet's been turned on inside of me.

"Hey, now," Thomas says, walking over and pulling me into his big embrace.

My tears get his t-shirt all wet, and I start to apologize, but he shushes me, rubbing the back of my hair. "I'm sorry for the hurt."

"I'll get over it," I say.

"You're strong like that," he agrees.

I want to tell him that I don't want to be strong. I want to march down the hall to that bedroom, pound on the door and beg Holden to give what we'd both felt this morning and last night a shot.

But I don't. I just press my lips together and nod. Because, what else, really, is there for me to do?

♪

Holden

I stand under the shower spray way longer than I should, considering that Sarah is in my bedroom, waiting for me to come out. I let the water pummel my face into full-out awake until all threads of fatigue have dissolved.

When I can avoid it no more, I get out, dry off, put on sweat pants and a t-shirt, then open the bathroom door.

Sarah is sitting on the bed, her knees against her chest, arms wrapped tight around her legs, as if she is physically trying to hold herself together. She doesn't look at me, her gaze on her pink toenails. "Can you explain to me what just happened out there?" she finally asks.

"Nothing happened," I say, hearing the lack of conviction in my own voice.

She looks up at me then, and her blue eyes snap fire. "Holden Ashford, don't you dare play me. I deserve better than that from you. Who is she?"

"A girl hoping to make it in Nashville just like Thomas and me." I blow out a sigh and sit down on the edge of the bed. "Her car burned up on the side of the interstate. We stopped to help her, and that's how we met. That's it."

"That's it?" Sarah repeats, incredulous. "She's living in your apartment. How is that it?"

"She lost everything in her car. It made sense for us to help her out."

"I get that. And why were you out all last night with her?"

"Waiting at the pound to get Hank Junior out. Her dog. Thomas lost him while we were at work."

"We?"

"We got a job at the same restaurant."

17

Sarah folds her arms across her chest and stares at me hard. "I see. Wow. It sure didn't take long for you to forget all about me."

"That's not true."

"It seems like you're well on your way," she says, tears welling in her eyes.

My heart suddenly feels like it's been wrapped in one big rubber band, and I know I'm coming across as a jerk. Which considering what's been happening between CeCe and me, I guess I am. "Why did you change your mind about coming?" I ask, meeting her tearful gaze.

"I missed you," she says, and the words are so broken, so heartfelt that the wall of resistance inside me starts to crumble.

"I can't believe you drove through the night. You hate driving at night."

She nods. "Don't worry. I know it was stupid."

I feel like such an ass. I am an ass. "It wasn't stupid. I just wish you'd let me know you were comng."

"I wanted to surprise you."

And I can see that's exactly what she'd hoped to do. Just forty-eight hours ago, that would have made me ecstatic. Forty-eight hours ago, we would have already been in bed, making up for lost time.

But we're not. And we both know something feels different.

"I'm sorry, Sarah. It's been a long night. I'm just beat. I need some sleep."

"Do you want me to go?" she asks, her voice cracking a little.

I hear the question, and yet my response doesn't come immediately, as it should.

"Of course not," I say, but too many seconds have passed for me to be completely convincing. I know Sarah, and I know what she wants right now is to tell me to go to hell and leave as suddenly as she came. But I guess she's not ready to throw in the towel just yet, so she bites her lip and nods.

I open the bedroom door and call for Patsy. She trots down

the hallway, looking up at me with expectant brown eyes. "Come on, girl," I say. "Nap time."

Inside the bedroom, Patsy looks around, walks to the side of the bed and lies down, stretching out with her chin on her paws.

Sarah looks at her like some unidentified object just fell through the roof. "She's sleeping in here?" she says.

"Yeah," I say.

"But you know I don't like–"

"I know you've never been around dogs, and you think you don't like them."

"That's not at all fair, Holden," she says, her voice deliberately even.

"I have a dog now, Sarah," I say. "I'm hoping you'll like her once you get to know her."

"I never should have come here!" Sarah jumps off the bed and stomps into the bathroom, where she promptly slams the door.

I reach down and rub Patsy's head. I want to call Sarah back and reassure her that she did the right thing in coming. I want to. I just don't know if it would be the truth.

♪

CeCe

I should sleep.

But I can't. Don't. Won't. One of those, anyway. To close my eyes and invite sleep would be to open the current plug on my thoughts and let them come flooding in. And since I'm pretty sure I will drown in them, I opt for staying awake.

I do take a shower, and that helps wash away some of my fatigue. I try not to think about what Holden and Sarah are doing in the next room, and when my mind refuses to blank, I increase the cold water until I'm shivering and nearly blue.

When I walk back into the kitchen wearing jeans and a wet ponytail, Thomas looks up from a bowl of cereal and says, "Aren't you going to bed?"

"I don't like to sleep during the day."

"Me, either. Wanna walk over to Starbucks for a coffee? I'm meeting a couple people there."

I glance at Hank Junior who's snoozing on the sofa. "I don't really want to leave him yet."

"He can go with us. We can sit outside."

At this, I immediately agree, since the last thing I want is to stay in the apartment alone with Holden and Sarah. "If you're sure we won't be in the way."

"Course not. I think you'll like them, anyhow."

The Starbucks is only three blocks over from the apartment. We walk the short distance with Hank Junior on full sniff alert. He meets up with an elderly Pug and a regal Great Dane who both greet him like they're old friends.

We get there at just after ten and find a table on the outside patio where students from Vanderbilt sit in front of laptops, and a variety of music types talk on cell phones and text in between sips of the morning's blend.

Thomas waves at a girl standing by the main entrance. She waves back and walks over. "Hey," Thomas says while they hug.

"Adrienne Langley, this is CeCe MacKenzie," he says. "And her boy Hank Junior."

"Hey, CeCe," Adrienne says. "Hey, Hank." She bends down to rub him under the chin, and the look in her eyes tells me she's a dog-lover. I can't help but instantly like her.

"Nice to meet you," I say.

"You, too," she says, standing again. "Where's Holden?"

"He got a little detained this morning," Thomas says by way of explanation.

"Oh, I was hoping he would be here," Adrienne says, and I can see she's a verified member of Holden's ever-increasing female fan club.

A tall, dark-haired guy walks up behind her and hands her a coffee. "Tall, medium roast, sis."

"Thanks," she says, smiling at him. "Thomas, this is my brother J.B. J.B, Thomas and his friend CeCe."

J.B. shakes Thomas's hand and then settles his gaze on me. "Nice to meet you both."

He's about as good-looking as any guy I've ever met. If he were trying out for a movie role, he'd probably get it just because he's got that kind of longish, wavy hair that says box office instant success. I can't stop myself from blushing under his assessment. "You, too," I say.

"This table okay?" We pull out chairs, while Hank Junior settles himself in a slice of shade from a nearby tree, then stretches out like he's got sleep to catch up on.

"What's your pleasure, CeCe?" Thomas asks. "I'll go in and get us a cup."

"Tall blonde," I say.

"We are talking about coffee, right?" J.B. says with a grin.

"We are," Thomas says, giving him a look. "Be right back."

Adrienne pulls out a chair, and J. B. steps around to take the one between the two of us. He waits for us each to sit before sitting down.

"Where are you from, CeCe?" Adrienne looks at me and then takes a sip of her coffee.

"Virginia."

"All right," J.B. says.

"How 'bout y'all?" I ask, attempting to ignore the suggestive edge in his voice.

"North Carolina," Adrienne answers.

"How long have you been here?"

"Six months."

"And three days," J.B. adds.

"Made any headway?" I ask.

"Some, I think," Adrienne says. "We're playing out most nights. Audiences are getting bigger. Youtube hits for our videos are increasing. And we're getting ready to record a song that we're releasing under our own label."

"Cool," I say, feeling more than a little like the new guppy in the pond. "What's the song like?"

"It's actually one we wrote with Thomas's buddy Holden the last time they were in town. I'm so in love with it."

My stomach does an automatic dip at the sound of Holden's name, and my head is filled with an instant vision of Sarah stretched out alongside him in bed, their legs entwined–

"You know him?" J.B. asks, jerking my attention back to the present.

"He and Thomas kind of rescued me from the side of the Interstate a few days ago."

"Lucky them," J.B. says, flirtation at the edges of the comment.

"I'm not so sure they saw it that way."

"They're good guys," Adrienne says. "If you need rescuing, they're the ones you want riding up on the white horse."

J.B. rolls his eyes and slides down in his chair, crossing his arms across his nicely muscled chest. "That white hat thing can get kind of boring, don'tcha think?"

Adrienne looks at me and shakes her head. "Don't pay any attention to him. He likes bad girls."

"Hey now. Dissing your brother like that."

Adrienne pins him with a look. "You know it's true."

Before J.B. can answer, Thomas returns with the coffee, setting mine down in front of me.

"Thanks," I say, pulling out the chair beside me so he can sit down.

"I got Hank Junior a little cup of whipped cream," he says, and puts the cup down in front of him. Hank starts to lick, tentatively at first, and then with total enthusiasm. Thomas grins. "Thought you'd like that."

"He's going to be totally ruined," I say, even as I can't deny loving Thomas a little more each time he does something like this.

"He's yours?" J.B. directs the question to me.

"Yes," I say.

"Which one of you sings?" J.B. teases.

"He's got a good howl," I answer. "Sometimes, I'd say he's the better of the two of us."

"She's being modest," Thomas throws in. "She sings like an angel."

"Really?" Adrienne asks, and despite her smile, I hear the competitive lilt in the question.

"As you know you do, too, Adrienne," Thomas says, tipping his coffee cup at her in mock salute.

"Why, thank you, sir," she says, perking back up.

"So what is it you two wanted to talk about this morning?" Thomas asks, stretching his legs out in front of his chair.

"I was hoping Holden would be with you so we could all talk," Adrienne says, "but what we wanted to discuss was pitching both our acts to venues, kind of as a double header thing. J.B. and

I think we draw a similar crowd and that we might make more of an impact that way."

"And we were hoping to write some more songs together," J.B. throws in.

"How far out are y'all booked?" Thomas asks.

"A week," Adrienne and J.B. say in unison.

"Nothing like job security, is there?" Thomas asks, and we all smile.

"We're booked over at the Cocky Cow tonight. If y'all want to play before us, we've already cleared it with the manager."

"Cool," Thomas says. "I'll check with Holden. Text you in a bit?"

"Sure," Adrienne says. "We've got an appointment with a publisher in an hour. And I need to go spiff up."

"All right, then," Thomas says. "Check you later."

Adrienne and J.B. push back their chairs and stand. Thomas and I do the same, and I wake up Hank Junior who yawns and then follows me through the maze of tables.

Adrienne and Thomas step aside to say something to one another, and J.B. turns to me with a smile. "Would you be free for a drink after our gig tonight?"

Given my no doubt accurate impression of J.B. as a player, I start to say no. But then I get an instant visual of Sarah with Holden and wonder how I can possibly stay in the apartment with them. "Maybe," I hedge.

"How do I get that changed to a yes?" he asks, looking down at me with a grin that I am sure rarely fails him.

"Do you like dogs?" I ask.

He laughs then. "Not as much as girls. But yeah, I like dogs. Is that a prerequisite?"

"Definitely," I say.

"Not a problem," he says, still grinning. "So I'll see you tonight then?"

"Sure," I answer.

"Good." He waves and gets in the convertible VW Adrienne is driving.

During our walk back to the apartment, Thomas looks at me and says, "You gotta watch that guy."

"How so?" I ask.

"His own sister won't let her friends date him."

"Ouch."

"Did he ask you out?"

"Yes."

"And?"

"I said I'd have a drink with him."

"He's not your type, CeCe."

"I don't know if I have a type yet," I say.

"And if you're doing this to get back at Holden–"

"Holden has a girl friend," I interrupt.

"I can't deny that," he says. "But don't let that make you do something you'll regret."

"It's just a drink," I say.

"Most mistakes start out that way," he says. "Let me ask you this. Would you go out with him if Sarah hadn't shown up?"

I'd like to prove him wrong by answering with an immediate yes, but we both know I'd be lying. So I don't say anything. What would be the point?

♪

Holden

We get to the Cocky Cow at just before eight. Thomas had woken me up around four so we could practice before our set. Sarah's upset with me because she wanted to have dinner alone and talk, but talking is about the last thing I want to do with Sarah since I have no idea what to say.

She's sitting at a corner table now, nursing a diet Coke and looking as if she's sorry the idea of coming to Nashville ever occurred to her.

CeCe is helping us get set up, and we're avoiding each other as if both our lives depend on it. I'm trying not to notice the way J.B. is openly flirting with her, or the way she's smiling back at him as if she likes it.

Adrienne comes over and gives me a hug, telling me how much she loves the song we wrote together. "I can't wait to hear you sing it," I say.

"Be happy to give you a private show," she says with just enough teasing in her voice to call the offer a joke if pride needs saving.

I stop short of an answer when Thomas walks over and shakes his head. "I ain't envying your position, man."

I don't bother to ask him what he means. "I had no idea she was coming," I say.

"Yeah, but didn't she have the right to?"

"I'm not saying she didn't," I admit.

"You just weren't expecting CeCe," Thomas says.

"No. I wasn't expecting CeCe."

Thunder claps outside the building, loud enough to make itself heard above the pre-show music playing in the bar.

"Whoa," Thomas says. "They're calling for some serious storms."

Thomas taps his phone screen, looks at it for a moment and then says, "Weather.com shows a tornado watch for this area."

CeCe walks up, deliberately not looking at me. "Tornado watch?" she repeats.

"That ain't no good," Thomas says.

"It's just a watch," I say. "Probably nothing."

I meet eyes with CeCe then for the first time since this morning when Sarah had greeted us at the front door. Our gazes snag for a moment, and it feels like both of us have trouble glancing away.

"You got a song in you tonight, CeCe?" Thomas asks.

She looks at him and starts to shake her head.

"Aw, come on. Just one." He names a couple her uncle wrote.

"What about Sarah?" CeCe says. "She might want to sing with you tonight."

"We'll ask her," Thomas says, "but I'm not sure she's in a singing mood."

I give him a look that makes him duck and throw an air punch at me. CeCe looks uncomfortable and says, "You should ask her."

"This a private meeting, or can I sit in?"

J.B. strolls over, one thumb hooked through the belt loop of his jeans, his gaze focused solely on CeCe.

"We're just trying to talk her into singing a song with us tonight."

"I'd sure like to hear you sing, CeCe," J.B. says, standing closer to her than seems necessary. "We still on for that drink tonight?"

"Yeah," she replies. "If we don't get hit by a tornado."

"Whhhhaat?" J.B. says.

"There's a watch," Thomas throws out.

"This place got a cellar?" J.B. asks, and from the look on his face, I'm thinking he's really worried about it.

"Shouldn't we be hitting the stage?" I say to Thomas.

"Eight o'clock. I reckon so," Thomas says.

"CeCe, you wanna hang out until Adrienne and I go on?" J.B. says.

"Sure," she answers, and if you ask me, her voice is a little too bright to be believable. Even so, her answer leaves me wishing I could remove the satisfied grin from J.B. Langley's mouth.

♪

CeCe

I know Holden and Sarah aren't talking. She's sitting at the back of the room, alternating staring at me with staring at him.

I'd like to go on and decide that I just plain don't like her, but then I think what it must be like to come all this way to see your boyfriend only to get here and realize that something's changed in the few days you've been apart.

I'm not saying that I think I'm responsible for that change. Maybe I'm just the bump in the road that's making Holden question whether he and Sarah are right for one another. But even I can see that he's questioning it.

I'm alternating between feeling like a rotten, relationship-wrecker and a hopeful, crush-stricken adolescent.

I sit at a table near the front of the room with J.B., nursing a Coke while Holden and Thomas bring the crowd of people in the room to life. Just about every person there is listening with the kind of intensity you only get when people really like what you're doing.

Without doubt, Thomas was born to be on stage. There's a natural ease to the way he tells something funny or revealing about himself and then segues into a song Holden has written about that exact thing. I could listen to them all night. Not just Thomas's voice but the way Holden plays the guitar as if it is the only thing he was ever meant to do. As if he feels every note. Every word. I find myself waiting for the moments when he comes in with a background vocal, his voice the perfect accompaniment to Thomas's thick, country twang.

I try not to meet eyes with them throughout the performance, but it's like there's a magnet between us. Every time I feel him looking at me, I can't help myself from letting my gaze bump his.

J.B. is apparently aware of this because every time it happens,

31

he leans forward and says something in my ear. I get the impression that he's doing it as much to rile Holden as he is to sweet talk me.

Thomas is talking to the crowd again. I pull my thoughts back to his voice, telling myself I'm not going to look at Holden again.

"This next number, folks," Thomas says, "is a song Holden wrote one night when we both decided we didn't really care what we had to do to support our love for this business, singing and writing songs. Short of armed robbery, of course."

Laughter ripples through the crowd.

"Aside from that, anything we did, whether it's building a house or waiting tables would just be the means to the freedom to do what we love. This here's called A Hammer and a Song."

I listen to the words, and I hear Holden in each and every one of them. He has a real gift, and it's clear that this life means everything to him. I can only imagine how hard that must have been for Sarah to accept. If she has.

When the song is over, a few beats of silence follow the moment when Thomas lays down his microphone. The applause erupts all at once, punctuated by whistles and whoops. I glance at J.B. whose clapping is tentative to say the least, his voice a little clipped when he says, "That's good stuff."

"It is," I say, and then before I know it, Thomas is taking my hand and pulling me up on the stage. My heart is beating a thousand miles an hour and my hands are suddenly clammy. Thomas tells the audience about my Uncle Dobie and the great songs he had written.

"We're gonna do one of those for you, folks," he says, nodding at me.

I close my eyes and wait for Holden's intro, and then Thomas and I dip into the song together. For the next three minutes, I'm in that other place where all that matters is the music. It's a place I sometimes wish I could stay in, that sweet spot where the notes and the words all come together to create something wonderful, magical.

When it's over, the crowd gives us their approval with gratifying applause. My heart is no longer racing, and I just feel grateful to Thomas for his generosity. I hug him. He hugs me back while the audience claps harder, and I force myself not to look at Holden.

We're about to leave the stage when a sudden noise rises above the clapping. Everyone goes silent, and the sudden wail of an alarm fills the room, the noise clogging our ears like smoke in the lungs.

A man in a white shirt and black pants runs over to the stage and takes the microphone from Thomas. "Folks, I'm the manager here. A tornado has just been spotted in the downtown area. We have been advised by public safety officials to immediately take cover in the downstairs part of the building. Let's all keep our cool. Single file if you would, and follow me to the stairwell."

His voice is even and reassuring as if this is something he does every night. He steps off the stage then and heads for the main entrance to the bar.

"Seriously?" Thomas says, looking at me and then Holden.

Holden glances at the back of the room and says, "I'll get Sarah. Meet you two downstairs."

He steps down from the stage and begins winding his way through the crowd to the back of the room where Sarah stands waiting, with a panicked look on her face.

I remember then that Hank Junior and Patsy are at the apartment alone.

"The dogs, Thomas," I say, feeling a well of panic. "I need to get home."

"CeCe, that siren means we need to do what they say. I'll drive you myself as soon as we get the all clear." Thomas takes my hand, and I follow him through the lobby to the stairwell where people are hurrying downstairs.

"They'll be all right," he says over his shoulder. "And look at it this way. This will probably give us something to write about."

"Then I hope it's a song with a happy ending," I say, tears welling up.

The alarm is loud, and I'd like to cover my ears as we head down, but I'm afraid to let go of Thomas's hand. My heart is throbbing in time with the siren's wail, and I say a silent prayer that this will be over soon.

The room we're filing into is large and dimly lit. The alarm has lost its knife edge blare, and I feel like I can again think a little more clearly. We find a spot in a far corner and sit on the floor against the wall.

I see Holden come through the door, Sarah holding onto his arm. I wish for a moment that they would sit at the opposite end of the room from us, but Thomas waves them over.

Holden looks at me and says, "Think the dogs will be all right?"

"I hope so," I say, not quite able to meet his concerned gaze.

"Why wouldn't they be?" Sarah asks. "They're inside, aren't they?"

No one answers her. I'm certainly not going to since what I want to say isn't likely to make us fast friends.

Holden takes the spot next to me, leaning back against the wall. Sarah studies him for a moment, then wilts onto the floor beside him, as if it is the last place on earth she wants to be.

"How long do we have to stay here?" she asks, the words sounding like those of a petulant seven-year-old.

"Until the threat of a tornado passes, I would imagine," Thomas says, and I can hear the disapproval in his voice.

The lights in the room, already dim, flicker and extinguish all together as if someone has just blown out a candle.

Voices rise up in protest, and then that of the manager calling out for everyone to please listen. "Sorry about that, folks. Looks like we've lost our power. I know none of you came out expecting this tonight. But for the moment, it is what it is. I doubt the lights will be out for long. Let's sit tight, and give this cloud a chance to pass on over. Oh, and keep your hands to yourself, please."

This actually pulls forth a chuckle from the crowd, although I notice Sarah doesn't laugh.

From our basement haven, the wind is muffled, but its fury is still evident. I can hear something flapping at the top of the stairs.

"Sounds like a door," Thomas says.

The sounds stops, and for a second, it's silent. And then out of nowhere, another sound hits, like a train speeding through the darkness. The roar is so loud I put my hands to my ears and squeeze hard. I scream and realize I'm not the only one. An arm encircles me from either side, both Thomas and Holden are holding onto me. I feel Sarah's arms bolt around Holden's waist, the four of us linked together like a human chain of fear.

I press my face into Holden's shoulder and bite back the terror that yanks me under like a sudden, unexpected riptide.

I want to melt into him, and here in the dark, I let myself imagine we are the only two here. I remember what it felt like to be in his arms, his mouth on mine, his hands–

But we're not alone. Sarah is crying now, and Holden is soothing her with his voice, telling her it'll be over soon, that everything is going to be all right.

I pull myself out of the half circle of his arm, and Thomas hooks me up against him, comforting me with his big embrace.

I'm not sure how long we sit there. It really seems like hours, but it might just be minutes. Or even seconds.

As quickly as the roar descended, it is gone. Just like that. In the snap of a finger. And the room is terrifyingly quiet.

"Is everyone all right?" the manager speaks up, his voice by now familiar even though we can't see him. He sounds shaken, as if he's not sure what to do next.

A chorus of yes, yes, yes rises up, followed by sighs of relief.

As if in unspoken agreement, everyone stays seated for a couple of minutes. No alarms. No wind. Just silence.

And then footsteps sound on the stairs, followed by an official-sounding voice. "Anyone need help down here?"

"I think we're all okay," the manager answers back. "Is it all right to come out?"

"Yes. Your building held up well. But it's a mess outside. Y'all be careful now. I brought some flashlights for you."

"Thanks," the manager says. He turns one on and shines it across the room.

I squint at the light, my eyes already adjusting to the dark. Thomas stands and offers me a hand. I get to my feet and say, "Can we go home now?" And I'm praying the tornado didn't hit our apartment building.

Thomas flicks on the flashlight someone just handed him and says, "Let's go."

Holden and Sarah follow us up the stairs. It's slow going with all the people in front of us, but we finally reach the top and walk out into the night.

A few street lights are on, others hanging limply from their poles as if they'd just taken a left hook. But that's the least of it. The four of us stand staring at the wreckage around us. Cars that had been parallel parked in front of the bar now sit on their sides, front end, and some are even rolled over on their tops.

It's like a giant lumbered down the street and picked them each up the way a toddler picks up toy cars, dropping them where he pleases when they cease to interest him.

No one says anything for a full minute, and then Thomas utters, "Good day in the mornin'."

"Let's go see if the truck is in one piece," Holden says.

We weave our way down the sidewalk to the side parking lot where Thomas had parked earlier. Amazingly enough, every car in the square lot is exactly as it had been left. The funnel cloud had made a line of carnage straight down the street, taking complete mercy on anything to either side of it.

"Thank goodness," I say.

"The only question," Holden says, "is will we be able to get out of here?"

Thomas glances around and nods once. "I didn't get her in four wheel drive for nothing."

"You can't just roll over other cars," Sarah says, sounding a little dazed.

"Y'all hop on in, and leave the driving to me," Thomas advises. And since we don't have any other choice, we do.

♪

Holden

CeCe and Sarah sit between Thomas and me, Sarah's back ramrod straight. I can see CeCe's trying her best not to touch shoulders with Sarah, but that's pretty much impossible since we're packed in here like books on a library shelf.

Sarah has her fingers entwined tightly with mine. I'm not sure if it's because she needs the security of my touch or if she's making a statement.

Not that CeCe appears to notice. She hasn't looked at me once since we came out of the basement. Even so, there's a cord of electricity between us that I feel and somehow know she does, too.

Thomas navigates the truck out of the parking lot and then rides with two tires on the sidewalk for a couple of blocks or so until we get around some of the vehicles that have been tossed along the street like toys.

A few people are standing outside shop doors looking shell-shocked. Thomas rolls down his window and throws out, "Y'all need any help?"

"We're good," a man answers back.

Most of the street lights are out, and it feels like a scene from one of those apocalyptic movies. The sky is still a heavy, gunmetal grey. We make decent headway until we're a couple of miles or so from the apartment. A Range Rover sits at an odd angle in the middle of the street, the driver's side door open. There's no one else anywhere in sight.

Thomas brakes the truck to a stop, and we both jump out and run to the car. There's a woman in the driver's seat. She's slumped to one side, unconscious. I realize then that it's Lauren, my boss at the restaurant.

Sarah and CeCe run over to the car. "What happened?" CeCe asks.

Before I can answer, CeCe spots Lauren and says, "Oh, no."

"Who is she?" Sarah asks.

"She owns the restaurant where we work," I answer. I lean in to feel for a pulse in her neck, my own heart pounding so hard I can hear it in my ears.

The beat is there, and I feel a quick jab of relief.

"Should we try to get her out?" Thomas asks.

"I don't know," I say, pulling my phone from my back pocket and dialing 911. An operator answers immediately and asks what my emergency is. I tell her, and she tells me the wait may be fifteen minutes or more because of the tornado and the number of emergency calls it has generated. She asks if we can get Lauren to the hospital.

"Yes," I say. "Or at least I think so."

"Call back if you can't," she says, and she's gone.

I look at Thomas and CeCe. "We need to get her to the emergency room."

"Can you take her vehicle, and I'll head for the apartment to check on the dogs?"

"Yeah," I say.

"Let's put her in the back," Thomas says. He leans in and lifts Lauren out like she's nothing more than a cotton ball and places her gently on the leather seat.

"CeCe, can you ride with her?" I ask. "At least if she wakes up, she'll know you."

"I'm going with Thomas," Sarah says, folding her arms and walking stiff-backed to the truck.

I start to go after her, tell her to come with us, but I honestly don't feel like arguing right now. And I'm also afraid of what might happen if we don't get Lauren to the hospital asap.

"Y'all get going. I'll take care of her," Thomas says, giving me a sympathetic look.

I get in the driver's seat, glance over my shoulder at CeCe

who is looking a little too pale, then throw the Rover into gear. I gun it for the hospital, reminding myself how to get there.

An iPhone is lying on the passenger seat. I pick it up and check the recent calls. There's Case Phillips's name and number.

I hold it up and flash the screen at CeCe. "Think we ought to call him?"

"Can't hurt. Maybe he'll know what might be wrong."

I hit send, and put it on speaker, unable to believe I'm actually calling Case Phillips.

He answers on the first ring. "Hey, baby. Are you okay? I've been trying to call you."

I clear my throat and say, "Mr. Phillips. This is Holden Ashford. I work for Lauren at the restaurant. We found her in her car, unconscious. My friend and I are driving her to the hospital, but we thought you might have an idea what could be wrong."

"She's diabetic," he says with quick urgency. "She's passed out before. There should be a kit in her purse."

"I already looked for her purse," CeCe says from the back seat. "There isn't one in the car."

"She never goes anywhere without it," Case says, disbelieving. "Could she have been mugged?"

"It's possible," I say. "The door was open when we pulled up."

Case lets out a string of curses and then says, "Keep me on the phone until you reach the hospital."

"Okay," I agree, and then put my attention on getting us there without wrecking.

I drive well over the speed limit, deciding I'll take my chances with an explanation if I get pulled over. Right now, all I care about is getting Lauren to the ER where someone will know how to help her.

We're there in minutes, and I pull up to the main door, hopping out and running inside. I'm still holding Lauren's phone, and I let Case know we made it.

"I'm driving now. I'll meet you there," he says. "Oh, and thank you. Thank you so much."

I click off the phone, realizing that he really loves her, the fear in his voice proof of it.

I flag down a nurse and tell her what's happened and that Lauren is diabetic.

She grabs a gurney and follows me back outside where I lift Lauren out of the seat and place her carefully on it.

"Are you family?" the nurse asks me.

"No," I say. "We found her like this in her car."

"Is there someone who can give us a history?"

"Her—Case Phillips," I say. "He's on his way."

The woman's eyes widen a little before professionalism slips back into place. "Please direct him to the registration desk when he gets here," she says, and then she's wheeling Lauren toward the ER doors marked Restricted.

I let myself look at CeCe then. She's still looking a little panicky.

"Will she be all right?" she asks, clearly needing me to say yes.

"I hope so," I say and realize that's the best I can do.

We find a parking place for the Rover and then walk back inside the hospital where we wait by a vending machine. In less than five minutes, Case Phillips runs through the main doors. I wave at him, and he walks over, his face drawn with worry.

"We're the ones who brought Lauren in," I say.

"Oh. Thank you. Thank you so much. Where is she?"

I point to the restricted door. "They took her in there. The nurse asked me to tell you they'll need whatever information you can give them."

"Of course." He glances at CeCe and then back at me again. "You both look familiar. Have we met?"

"Sort of," I say, not wanting to elaborate.

But his face lights with recognition and then slight

embarrassment. He glances at CeCe and says, "Ah, sorry about that."

She shakes her head. "Don't worry about it."

By now, people are starting to recognize him. There's some pointing and murmuring, a couple of giggles.

"Do you two have a ride?" he asks.

"We can get a cab," I say.

"No need. Take the Rover. We'll get it later."

"No, really."

"I insist," he says. "And Lauren would as well."

"All right," I say, still reluctant.

"I better get them what they need so I can see her."

"Sure."

"Thank you both again."

He heads for the registration desk, stares and smiles following him. And if it weren't a hospital, I'm sure people would be asking for autographs.

CeCe and I walk to the parking lot with a few feet of space between us, silent.

I unlock the Rover and slide into the driver's side. For a moment, I think she's going to get in the back again, but she opens the passenger door with some reluctance.

"I don't bite," I say.

"Hm," she says on a note of disagreement.

I back out of the parking lot and pull onto the street, the Rover engine an expensive sounding low rumble.

"I hope she'll be okay," CeCe says, looking out the window. "My mom nearly died once like that."

"I'm sorry," I say, glancing at her. "Were you there?"

"I found her when I got home from school."

"That must have been scary."

"It was," she says.

"Do you miss her?"

"A lot."

"What about your dad?" I ask.

"He's never been in the picture."

For some reason, this surprises me.

"Your parents?"

"Divorced. My mom actually lives in London."

"Do you see her often?"

"Not very."

"And your dad?"

"He's in Georgia. We pretty much try to avoid each other."

"That's sad," CeCe says and then looks as if she wants to take it back.

"Yeah, it is," I agree.

"Is it anything that can't be fixed?"

"Probably."

She wants to ask more. I can feel it. But I guess she senses I don't want to talk about it. We're quiet for a few moments, and then I say, "CeCe?"

"Hmm?"

"About Sarah."

"Don't. Please," she says, holding up a hand. "You don't need to. It's not like I didn't know you had a girlfriend."

"I didn't mean for this to happen," I say. "I'm not a guy who does that kind of thing."

"And I'm not a girl who does that kind of thing. So we need to forget about it."

"I want to," I say. "I just don't know if I can."

She looks at me then, and I see the quick flash of longing. It echoes inside me, and I swing the Rover off the street into a parking place. I turn off the engine, and we sit like this, staring straight ahead while I tell myself I'm being an idiot. That I should drive us both home. Now.

That doesn't explain why I turn to her, slip my hand to the back of her neck and pull her to me. I don't know who kisses who first. But it doesn't really matter. I can't think of anything else. I don't want anything else. Just her mouth beneath mine. And those sweet, soft sounds she's making, blocking out any other thoughts.

She slips her arms around my neck, and even with the gear shift between us, we manage to melt into one another. I've never wanted anyone in my life the way I want her now. I can't separate the want from my heartbeat, my breathing; it's so much a part of me.

It's no surprise that she's the one to pull away first. She opens the Rover door and jumps out as if it's the only sure ticket to safety. I sit for a moment, my eyes closed as I force myself to rational thought.

I let a few moments pass, then get out and walk around the vehicle where CeCe is leaning against a big round oak tree.

"We know better," she says.

"I don't deny that."

"That won't happen again," she adds, and I can't tell if she's trying to convince me or herself.

"CeCe–"

"You have someone in your life," she goes on as if I haven't spoken. "As long as that's the case, we can't be."

I know she's right. I want to argue, disagree, throw out excuses. But there really aren't any. "I'm sorry," I say, the words limp and meaningless.

We stare at each other for a string of seconds, and I feel like I'm about to lose something I never knew I was looking for. I jab the toe of my boot into the sidewalk, and wish I had an argument to stand on. But I don't. And we both know it.

"Can you give me a little time?" I ask.

"To what? Figure out how to break her heart into a hundred pieces instead of a thousand."

"No–"

"*Yes*, Holden. She loves you. And you probably still love her, too."

I'd like to deny it outright, tell her she's wrong. A few days ago, though, I did love her. Or thought I did.

"I don't want to be the reason you hurt her, Holden. If what you have isn't real, then it shouldn't take me to help you figure that out. And if it is real, well, it's real."

She stares at me for a few heartbeats, and I know I could sway her. Just by reaching out and pulling her to me. I also know that would make me the biggest kind of jerk. And probably a fool as well. Because she's right.

CeCe gets back in the Rover, buckles her seat belt.

I walk around and slide in the driver's side, pulling out onto the street. I hit the Satellite radio button, and music fills the interior. It's loud, and I like it that way. It keeps what I'm thinking inside of me. Silent. As it should be.

♪

CeCe

It's after one a.m. when we let ourselves in the door of the apartment.

Hank Junior greets us in his usual way, jumping down from the sofa and trotting to the door to first nudge me with his nose and then Holden. Loyalty keeps him from going to Holden first, even though I suspect, if he had his way, he would.

Ever since we sprang him from the pound, Hank Junior looks at Holden the way he's always looked at me. Like he knows most of the secrets to the universe.

Patsy's still more cautious. She waits for Holden to walk over to the couch and rub her under the chin. With this reminder that he's one of the nice guys, she's suddenly all wiggles and wags, hopping down to trot into the kitchen after him and Hank Junior.

I hear the refrigerator door open and the rustling of the plastic wrapping that holds the sliced turkey Holden gives Hank Junior and Patsy every night when we get home from the restaurant.

"Holden?"

I jump at the sound of Sarah's voice from the end of the hall, and reality comes crashing back like a cold ocean wave.

I call for Hank Junior and head for my room, my only regret that I have to pass Sarah on the way. She avoids my eyes on the way to the kitchen, and I step into the bedroom, wait for Hank to pad in behind me and close the door. I flip on the light and spot Thomas sprawled on the floor next to the bed in a sleeping bag.

"Hey," he says, raising up on one elbow. "Hope you don't mind me crashing in here."

"Of course not," I say. "You take the bed, Thomas. I'll be fine on the floor."

"Not necessary. Unless you wanna share it?" he says with a teasing grin.

His hair is all messed up, and there's a smile in his eyes. It occurs to me then that some girl is going to fall madly in love with him. For a second, I wish it were me. "You would so regret that in the morning," I say, heading into the bathroom.

"I'm thinking you might be wrong about that."

"You're just being nice to me," I say, putting toothpaste on my toothbrush.

"How you figure?"

"Because I was dumb enough to fall for Holden."

"Apparently, you're not aware of your obvious charms, sweetheart," he says.

I smile. "Thanks. My ego could use the boost right about now."

"He's not rejecting you, CeCe. It's just–"

"Sarah was there first," I finish for him.

"Yeah. I guess," he says.

"I get it."

"Doesn't make it hurt less though, does it?"

"No, it doesn't." I reach for my nightgown where it hangs on a hook behind the door. I push the door closed and slip out of my clothes.

I flick off the bedroom light before making my way to the bed, sliding under the covers, Hank already curled up at the foot.

A car drives by on the street outside the bedroom window, and then the room is silent again.

"Have you ever been in love, Thomas?"

"I thought it was love," he says.

"It wasn't?"

"If it doesn't last, I don't guess you can call it love."

"Yeah," I say.

"Felt good at the time though," he adds. "And I got a pretty good tune out of it. Holden got tired of seeing me mope around, so he made me write a song with him about her."

I laugh softly. "What was it called?"

"Fifty Acres and a Tractor."

"Seriously?"

He laughs. "Holden has a way of clarifying the picture."

At the mention of his name, I picture Sarah and him in the other room. I wonder if he's making love to her, and the thought is so painful, I squeeze my eyes closed tight to disrupt the image. "Thomas?"

"Yeah?"

"Can I come down there with you?"

"Well, sure. We'll both the do the sleeping bag thing. Let Hank have the bed."

I never had a brother. Never imagined what it would feel like to have someone in my life who might have my back the way a brother would. But I'd like to think he would have been like Thomas if I did have one.

I slide out of bed and scoot into the bag beside him. He raises up so I can rest my head on his shoulder. He rubs his thumb across my hair, and I know he's guessed what I'm thinking about.

"You know it'll work out how it's meant to," he says.

I nod, unable to force any words past the lump in my throat.

"Meanwhile, you got a singing career to work on."

"And starting tomorrow morning, that's all I'm going to think about. Forget this love stuff."

"There you go. It just gets in the way, anyhow."

Hank starts to snore, and we both laugh.

"I'm glad I met you, Thomas," I say.

"I'm glad I met you, CeCe," he agrees.

He gives me a kiss on the top of my head, and we let ourselves fall asleep.

♪

THE KNOCK THAT wakes us up is sharp and a little angry-sounding.

I raise up on one elbow at the same time Thomas does, and we knock heads, both of us muttering a groggy, "Ouch."

"Yeah?" Thomas barks out.

The door opens a crack, and Holden sticks his head inside. He looks from one of us to the other, his eyes going wide, before he says, "Seriously?"

Thomas rakes a hand over his face, and gives him a glare. "Don't get your panties in a bunch, man. What do you want?"

Holden looks as if he wants to slam the door and rewind these last few moments. "Lauren called, CeCe. She wants us to bring the Rover over to her house."

"When?" I ask, sleep still at the edges of my voice.

"Now."

"Why?"

"I don't know."

"Can't you take it without me?"

"She specifically said to make sure you come, too. If we want a job to go to tonight, we probably oughta do as she asks."

I roll over on my knees, arch my back like a cat and shake loose the threads of fatigue. When I flop back over, Holden is staring at me like I'm the glass of water he's crossed a desert for.

"I'm going back to sleep," Thomas says and yanks the sleeping bag over his head, leaving me bare-legged and exposed to Holden's caught-in-the-headlights stare.

"Okay," I say. "I'll be ready in ten minutes."

He closes the door without responding. I scramble to my feet, yank a t-shirt on over my head and hook a leash to Hank Junior's collar.

We head outside into the cool morning air, and goosebumps instantly break across my arms. Hank makes short work of his business. I'm ready to go back in when Holden comes out with Patsy.

Awkward doesn't begin to describe the cloud that instantly descends over the two of us. He walks Patsy over to a spot of grass near Hank and me. He's dying to ask. I can see it in his face. I have no desire to rid him of his misery, but even so, I say, "You know your best friend better than that, don't you?"

Red tints his cheeks before he says, "Yeah."

"Then why would you even think. . . ."

"Who you sleep with really isn't any of my business anyway, is it?" he asks, his voice sharp.

"As a matter of fact, no, it isn't," I say.

"With Sarah in your bed, I don't know why you would care who's in mine." The words aren't nearly as neutral sounding as I'd intended them to be.

I don't wait for him to respond. I hightail it back up the stairs and into the apartment, slapping the door closed behind me. I let the shower water run a little extra cold this morning, more to cool my anger than to wake me up. In a few short minutes, I'm dressed, and waiting outside by the Range Rover, my hair pulled back in a wet ponytail.

When Holden comes out, he's wearing a lime green shirt that makes him look so darn good I could cry at the realization that I have fallen for a guy I am never going to have.

He walks – strides or stomps might be more accurate – around to the driver's side, hits the remote and slides in. I get in, too, and we ride the first couple of miles without speaking.

"Coffee?" he says in a neutral voice.

I nod.

He swings into a Starbucks drive-through and orders two tall breakfast blends, remembering to ask for mine the way I like it. The consideration dings my anger, and I feel it leak out of me like helium from a week old balloon.

I hand him money for my coffee. When he ignores me, I drop it in the cupholder and look out the window. We sip in silence.

Holden drives away from the city, and it isn't long before the urban roads become rural. Enormous houses begin to appear on either side of the road, wide green pastures defined by white board fencing. Horses graze the fields with lazy selectivity, as if food is plentiful and they are merely indulging their host. It's as beautiful a place as any I've ever seen anywhere. I wish the mail boxes had names on them and imagine they would read like Urban, Paisley, Parton, and Keith.

I want to comment on how amazing they are but force myself not to since we seem to be in a contest of who can hold out the silence the longest. But when the GPS on Holden's phone indicates we should make a right turn onto an asphalt driveway lined by white fencing that stretches out as far as we can see, I can't help but gasp my delight.

"Incredible!" I say.

"Yeah," Holden agrees.

A half mile or so, and a house comes into sight. It sits on a high knoll, golf course green grass cascading down to meet the pasture fencing.

"Is this Lauren's house?" I ask.

"I don't know," Holden says. "All she told me was the address."

We pull into the circular driveway, and Holden cuts the engine. The massive wood front door opens, and Case Phillips steps out. Holden and I both glance at each other like tongue-tied teenagers.

He steps out onto the stoop in bare feet and blue jeans, a t-shirt that reads *Country Boys Get the Row Hoed* stretching the width of his impressively honed chest. I'm starstruck, no point in denying it. I was lucky enough to see him in concert on my sixteenth birthday, and my mama had spent a good portion of her week's paycheck to get us on the third row. I'd sat there in a near trance-like state, listening to him woo every female in the place – including my mama – with the voice that had given him number one single after number one single.

And now I'm sitting here in front of his house. Whoa.

Case waves us out of the vehicle. We open the doors and get out our respective sides.

"Y'all come on in," he says and disappears back inside the house.

Holden and I look at each other with wide eyes, and I can tell he's as awed as I am. We bump shoulders going through the front door. Holden steps to one side and then closes it behind us.

There's music playing from a room ahead of us. Surprisingly, it's not country. It's pop with a heavy beat. A giant winding staircase sits to our right. The ceiling is high and open, and oil paintings line the walls that curve around and up.

I feel a little like Alice in Wonderland and have to force myself not to sidle up next to Holden as I would like to. He leads the way through the foyer toward the music, and we end up at the entrance to a very large room lined with bookcases on one wall and four big screen TVs on the opposite one.

There must be a dozen oversize leather chairs with matching ottomans scattered across the room. Sitting in one with her feet tucked up beneath her is Lauren.

She has a mug in one hand, a book in the other. "Hey," she says, looking up at us.

Case walks over to a wall unit and turns a button. The music lowers to barely audible.

"How are you?" I ask, thinking she still looks a little pale.

"Good," she says. "Thanks to the both of you."

Holden and I glance at each other, neither of us comfortable with the praise.

"Would y'all like some coffee or something?" Case asks, dropping down into the leather chair next to Lauren.

"No, thank you," we say in unison, and I think maybe we're starting to look and sound like twin puppets.

"Y'all sit down then," Case says and waves a hand at two chairs opposite theirs.

Holden and I sit, again puppet-like.

"So what's your story?" Case asks, his blue eyes direct on us both.

"Ah, I'm not sure what–" Holden begins.

"Why are you two in Nashville?" Case says. "Music I'm assuming."

We both nod, and Case and Lauren smile.

"Relax, y'all," Lauren says. "I know you two aren't this uptight at the restaurant."

I make an effort to do exactly that just because I feel so foolish sitting here like a bowling pin. I let my shoulders dip in and sit back in the chair.

"What's your plan for making it here?" Case asks. "You write? Sing? Play?"

"I write," Holden replies. "Sing a little."

"I sing," I say.

"I have a partner I play with," Holden adds.

"Look, the reason we called y'all over this morning," Case says, "is first to thank you for what you did for Lauren." He reaches over and takes her hand in his. I realize then that in spite of the scene we witnessed in Lauren's office, the two of them are no casual thing. They have real feelings for one another. That actually makes me happy for Lauren, even though I am one of the countless thousands of females who have no doubt had illicit dreams about him.

"If you hadn't stopped to help her–" He breaks off, squeezes her hand and then looks at us again. "Thank you."

I nod.

"I'm glad we could," Holden says.

"So when Lauren said you were both wanting to get into the music business, I thought I'd put this in front of you first. No guarantees it'll work or you'll be what I'm looking for, but even a shot is hard to come by in this town."

My heart kicks up to a level I can hear in my ears. *Thrump-ush. Thrump-ush.*

"I'm looking to develop a young group. Three or four

members, raw talent in place but with the ability to still be shaped. That fit y'all at all?"

I'm actually holding my breath. Waiting for Holden to say I'm not part of his and Thomas's gig. But that's not what he says. "Absolutely," he answers, and I feel my chest release like an air valve has just been turned. I look at him with the most neutral expression I can muster, waiting to hear what he's going to say next. "We'd be really grateful to have the chance to play for you, Mr. Phillips."

"It's Case," he says. And then, "Two guys and two girls is what I'd planned to look at putting together. You got someone in mind for that?"

Holden answers without hesitating. "We do."

"All right then," Case says, slapping his hands on his thighs and standing. "Y'all come back around five this afternoon. I've got a studio here. We'll see what we come up with."

"I'll call the restaurant and get someone to take your shifts for tonight," Lauren says. "It won't be a problem."

"Thank you," I say, standing.

Holden gets to his feet and says, "Yeah, thank you so much. Both of you."

Case walks us to the door, pulls it open and once we've stepped outside, says, "Really. You have no idea how much I appreciate what you did for her last night. I can't imagine–"

"It was our pleasure," Holden says. "And you know, you don't have to do this for us just because–"

"I know I don't," he says. "But I want to."

There's a cab waiting out front by the Rover, and I realize he must have already had that arranged.

"The fare's taken care of," he says. "See you at five."

And with that, he goes back inside the house.

♪

Holden

"What exactly just happened?" I ask as we roll down the long driveway toward the main road.

"I'm still wondering myself," CeCe says. "Did we just get the kind of break that people wait years for?"

"I think we did."

"But we're not actually a group," I say, starting to panic, "and how are we going to become one before five o'clock this afternoon?"

"I don't know, but we are," I say.

"Are you talking about Sarah as the fourth person?" CeCe asks.

"Yeah," I say, and just saying it out loud makes me realize how ridiculous it is to think that she'll even consider doing it. After the argument we'd had this morning before I left, it'll be amazing to me if she hasn't already left to drive back to Atlanta.

"Do you think she will?" CeCe asks.

"She has to," I say.

"What if she won't?"

"Let's not even think that right now."

"I really don't see her wanting to be on a stage with me."

She's right, but how can I admit that? We've just been handed an opportunity that we might never get again. Just to be heard by Case Phillips, not to mention being considered as a project he's willing to develop.

"Shouldn't you call Thomas?" CeCe asks.

I pull my phone from my pocket and tap the screen for his number. He answers with a groggy, "Hello?"

"Are you still in the sleeping bag?"

"What? You're speaking to me now?"

"Not out of choice," I say.

"Maturity never was your thing," he grumbles.

"You're not going to believe this, but Case Phillips just asked us to play for him this afternoon at five o'clock."

"What?"

Thomas is awake now. I smile. "He's looking to put together a group. The only thing we have to do before this afternoon is talk Sarah into auditioning with us."

"Oh, no problem," Thomas says, blowing out a sigh. "I'll run on over to Music Row and see if I can hunt down Miranda Lambert while I'm at it."

"She's still there, right?" I ask.

"*Somebody's* running the shower in your room."

"Good. Don't let her leave, okay. We'll be there in fifteen minutes."

"We've never all played together," CeCe says as I drop my phone in my shirt pocket.

"We've never all had an opportunity like this," I say. "It's like winning the lottery. How many times do you win the lottery?"

"Odds are never."

"Exactly," I say. I just hope I can convince Sarah of this.

♪

SHE'S AT THE DOOR with her suitcase when we get back.

"Where are you going?" I ask, as if I don't already know.

"Back to Atlanta," she says, glancing at CeCe and then forcing her gaze on me.

"Did Thomas tell you what just happened?" I ask.

"Yes. And I don't see what that has to do with me."

"We need you to audition with us, Sarah. He's looking for a group. Two guys. Two girls."

Sarah tightens her grip on her purse strap and says, "This has always been your dream. It was never mine. And I came here for you. Not to be part of some ridiculous rainbow-chasing."

The words cut. I can't deny it. I'm sure the wound shows on

my face, and I can feel CeCe and Thomas both looking at me with resignation, like they know she's never going to agree.

"Maybe it is, Sarah," I say. "But this is a chance that comes along about as often as the pot of gold. What do we have to lose in going for it? What do you have to lose?"

She looks at me for a long moment, and tears well in her eyes. "You," she says.

♪

CeCe

I'm not sure if I should clap or cry.

Holden doesn't look at me before he follows Sarah into the bedroom. Hank Junior and Patsy stare at me from the couch. Hank Junior jumps off and trots over to greet me with a body wag. Patsy thumps her tail but doesn't get down.

"You gonna consider that a victory or a defeat?" Thomas throws out from the kitchen where he's unloading the dishwasher.

"Victory," I say, walking over to help him.

"For the audition, yeah. Your heart, not so much."

"I'm taking my heart out of the equation."

"Easy said."

I want to say not really, but choose silence as a better alternative.

Within five minutes, Holden and Sarah walk into the kitchen. Her eyes are dry, and she looks resigned if not happy.

"We've got the rest of the day," Holden says, "to get three songs down dead and figure out how we're going to look like we've been playing together forever. Let's get on it."

♪

IF I WERE AN OUTSIDER looking in, I would have to give the four of us credit.

We do exactly what Holden said we would need to do and get down to business. We set up in the living room, Hank Junior and Patsy watching from their perch on the couch. Except for a couple breaks to take them outside and grab something to eat, we don't stop practicing.

We decide to go with two covers that everybody knows, a Rascal Flatts and a Faith Hill. On the Rascal Flatts, Thomas takes the lead, while Sarah and I do harmony. On the Faith Hill, I take a verse, Sarah takes another and Thomas joins us on the chorus.

The third song is an original of Holden's, and both he and Thomas decide that I should do the lead vocal. I feel the needles in Sarah's glare, but she actually doesn't say anything. She just goes along with every indication of being a team player. That is, until I butcher the fourth line of the first verse for the seventh or so time.

"Seriously?" She throws her hands up in the air, turns to Holden and says, "I know this song. Why is she singing it?"

She glances at me and then back at Holden. "You think she's better than I am?"

"You know that's not it," Holden says, rubbing the guitar pick between his thumb and index finger.

"Then what is it?" she asks.

Thomas shakes his head and starts to laugh. "Here's how I see it. By some stroke of good fortune," he says, nodding at me and then at Holden, "these two have managed to get us an opportunity that few people would ever get no matter how hard they worked their tails off in this town. Case Phillips wants to pay them back for pretty much saving the life of the woman he loves. And I for one am not gonna laugh in the face of that. I am totally content to ride shotgun on this one. Sarah. If I were you, I would be, too."

Sarah's fluster is immediately apparent in the red stain on her cheeks and the way her lips part as if she wants to say something, but is trying desperately hard to stop herself from doing so.

"If we get past this audition," Thomas says, "then we can look at shaking out some of the kinks that might be bothering either of us. But until then, I say spit shine the heck out of the pair of boots we've been offered to walk in. All in favor, say aye!"

No one actually gives a verbal assent, but we all nod our agreement. Sarah appears to put on emotional blinders for the rest of the session.

Three hours later, I can't believe where we are. We actually sound *really* good. Holden makes a recording on his computer and plays back what we have so far. I'm amazed at how we sound. Like we've been playing and singing together for ages. I'm not sure how that could actually be possible, but we do.

Even with all the undercurrents working so hard to pull us under, we somehow manage to rise above them, and our sound has something fresh and unique to it. I'm suddenly in love with it.

Sarah's voice is like honey, smooth and golden, fluid and flowing. My voice has grit to it, an edginess I've been told by some, that somehow synchs with Sarah's. Thomas has his own thing, a voice so big and rooted in country that the truth is he doesn't need either one of us to own the stage. I love listening to him, especially when he drops the melody for a Georgia infused rap that catches and holds the ear.

And I love the song itself.

Holden loves sound, and every line of music holds something so catchy that I know listeners will want to hear more.

It is four-fifteen by the time we put the last bit of polish on the song. We're supposed to be at Case Phillips's house at five, and neither of us has showered or changed yet.

I for one feel in need of a few minutes under the faucet to regroup and get a handle on the flutters of panic intent on welling up inside me.

We talk for a few moments about what to wear, agree that Sarah and I should opt for something simple and basic. I'm glad since I don't have a lot to choose from. Holden and Thomas agree on a light blue shirt and jeans.

In my room, I stand in front of the mirror and give myself a long hard look. From the corner of my eye, I catch Hank Junior staring at me from his spot on the bed. I shrug at him and say, "You know how I get before I sing. Well, this is like a million times more nervewracking than all the other times put together."

My sweet dog cocks his head to the right, his long Hound ear lifting like a question mark. "I know all the logical stuff. I've sung in front of people before. It's a waste of energy. You're right. But I can't help it."

I go over to the bed and sit down next to him, rubbing under his chin the way he likes me to. "This could be it, you know. This could be *the* only shot I get here. What if I'm not ready? I thought I would have all kinds of time to get better before anyone was really looking."

Hank lifts his head to lick my cheek. I lean over to give him a fierce hug. "I wish you could be there. That would make me feel better."

Hank rolls over on his side and bats me with one of his big paws as if to say, "You're being ridiculous."

"I know," I agree. "Suck it up, right?"

In the shower, I think about a book I read not too long ago on focus and how it can be the determining factor between people who are good at something and people who are great at something.

I admit it. I want to be great at singing.

I would never say this out loud because I know how it would sound. But deep down inside, I feel like I already am. Intellectually, I know how much growth I have ahead of me. But the depth and breadth and scope of my love for singing is so immeasurable that it feels like the very best part of me. Something that's good and pure. I've actually worried about what would happen to my love for music if I don't make it here. If I reach a point where I have to admit I'm never going to be able to make a living with my music. Concede defeat.

I haven't let myself think this very often because it's really too painful to consider. But I know it happens all the time. Every day in places like this, in L.A. and New York City. Kids who are drawn to the lure of fame, giving the dream everything they have. Only to find that the dream was only that. A dream.

Realizing that my thoughts are not exactly fuel for focus, I drop my head back and let the water pummel my face, beating the negativity out of me. I force myself to look at this as a gift, dropped from above, at random, perhaps, Holden and I the lucky recipients.

Something my pastor had said once in the church Mama and I went to when I was a little girl comes to me then. A gift is a wondrous thing. But it's the ways in which we share it that can give it wings.

I think about this in light of all the reasons why Holden, Thomas, Sarah, and I are such an unlikely match. And I know that if I let myself think about that for even a second longer, I'm going to waste something I may never be offered again.

And that's when I decide that no matter what happens on anyone else's part tonight, I'm going to give this everything I've got. If we fail, at least I'll know I gave it the very best I am currently capable of giving.

♪

AS A GROUP, we clean up pretty well.

We leave the dogs at the apartment and the four of us ride church-pew style out of Nashville central and into the countryside.

Thomas is driving and I'm sitting next to him, Sarah wedged in between Holden and me.

We're breaking the seat belt law. Holden had insisted he be the one to go without, even though I had argued without success to share one with Thomas. Admittedly, it would have been an interesting position necessary to make that work. Thomas and Holden had both laughed while Sarah merely rolled her eyes.

Once we table the seat belt discussion, we drive the remainder of the way to Case's house in silence. I think we're each doing what we need to do to get our best game on.

Again, we roll by estate after estate, and Thomas offers up several whistles of appreciation. Sarah's expression indicates she sees such magnificence every day of her life. Either that, or she doesn't want to let on she's impressed.

Thomas pulls up in the circular driveway, and we slide out, silent and solemn-faced. Holden lifts his guitar case from the truck bed. We walk in a straight line to the front door, Holden in the front, Thomas in the back, Sarah and I sandwiched in between.

Holden rings the doorbell, and a housekeeper answers. Dressed in a white uniform, her instant smile welcomes us. She's round-faced, round-hipped and warm as a butter biscuit. "Y'all come on in," she says. "Mr. Case is expecting you. Right this way."

She leads us through the enormous house, wood floors echoing our footsteps. At the far back right corner, she opens a heavy door behind which sits the most incredible recording studio I never thought to imagine. Red leather chairs are scattered about, dark walnut walls a backdrop to soundproofing boards disguised as artwork.

Behind an enormous recording desk sits Case Phillips and a man I don't recognize. Case stands, waves a hand at us and says, "Welcome. This is my producer Rhys Anderson. Rhys, I'll let these folks do their own introductions."

Holden shakes the other man's hand and says, "I'm Holden Ashford. This is Thomas Franklin. CeCe MacKenzie and Sarah Saxon."

The man shakes each of their hands, his smile genuine and also welcoming. "How y'all doing?" He looks smart, like someone who's been very successful in this business. His clothes agree with the assumption, his shirt and jeans carrying the stamp of some exclusive men's department.

"This here's my band," Case says, indicating the other five people in the room. "And that over there in the corner is my son Beck. He's sitting in for one of our guitar players tonight who's out sick. He might look young, but don't worry, he can hold his own."

We all smile, and Beck drops us a nod of greeting. He looks so much like his dad. No one would need to be told they were father and son. He meets my gaze and smiles, and I smile back.

"What'd y'all bring to sing tonight?" Case asks.

"Two covers and another song that I wrote," Holden says, his tone respectful and a little uncertain.

"How about we hear the original?" Case asks. "I'm lookin' to see who y'all are without the instant comparison to someone who might have sung a song before. Y'all come on in and get set up. You got a chord chart for these guys?"

"I do," Holden says, reaching inside his guitar case and pulling out the sheets.

"Good man," Case says.

The players glance at the sheets and almost immediately start to strum at the chords. Under their expertise, the song is instantly recognizable, and I notice the pleased look on Holden's face. I can't imagine what it must feel like to him, hearing people of this caliber playing a song he wrote.

"You'll be playing with them?" Rhys directs to Holden.

"Yeah, if that's okay."

"Sure, it is."

In less than fifteen minutes, Cases's guys have the song nailed and Rhys directs Sarah, Thomas, and me into the sound booth that runs along the outer wall of the room.

Sarah whispers something in Holden's ear, clinging to his arm like he's a buoy in the middle of a raging ocean. I almost feel sorry for her. It's clear that she's out of her element. Not that I'm brimming over with confidence. But maybe the difference is that I want this to be a success. And maybe she just wants to get through it.

Holden leans down and says something to her. She walks to the microphone, her expression set and uneasy.

The band runs through the song once without stopping, and I'm amazed at how it sounds like they've played it a hundred times before. Thomas, Sarah, and I wade into the melody with tentative effort. I feel their unease as part of my own. I will myself to block out everything except my role in this.

The band starts the song up again, and the three of us are a little more confident, but not much.

Case stands and holds up a hand, motioning for us to stop.

The music drops to silence, and we stop singing.

"Hey, look y'all," Case says, running a hand around the back of his neck. "The only way this is going to turn out worth a hoot is if you forget where you are. You're just singing in church back home with all your aunts and uncles. That's the you I want to hear. Okay?"

The three of us nod, mute, and I force the knot of pressure in between my shoulder blades to relent. I can't think about Thomas or Sarah and their own batch of nerves. I can only control my own. I close my eyes and picture what Case just described. The little Southern Baptist church where I grew up. The tiny pulpit from which our choir belted out old-fashioned gospel hymns every Sunday morning.

And I see myself performing solos when I was nine, the familiar faces of the congregation smiling up at me, the smell of the coffee brewing in the church kitchen wafting up into the sanctuary. The way rain pinged off the tin roof of the old building and how that sound became part of whatever music we were singing.

By going there, I forget all about the here and now. I'm just me. Singing like I always have. For the pure love of it. For the joy it makes me feel.

That's how the next several hours pass. I can hear that Thomas, and even Sarah, have found their own ways to shake off the stage fright and just sing.

It's nearly eleven p.m. when Rhys raises a hand and says, "I think we got it."

He sounds pleased, and relief washes through me.

Only then do I let myself come back to the present, the laughter and good-natured ribbing of the band members seeping into my awareness. I step out of the booth, and Cases's son, Beck, walks over and says, "Y'all rocked that."

I smile and shake my head. "Y'all made us look good."

"It seems like you've really got something," he says, his hands shoved in the pockets of his jeans, the smile on his face less confident than I would have expected from someone who'd grown up with a country music star as his father.

"Thanks," I say. "It's really an incredible opportunity."

"Yeah, well, my dad doesn't waste his time. So if he brought you here, he thought he had good reason."

I start to bring up the thing about Lauren, but decide against it since she isn't here tonight, and I'm not sure how public their relationship is.

Case walks over to the stainless steel refrigerator in one corner of the room, opens the door and starts passing out bottled beer. "If you're not old enough to legally drink this," he says, "then don't. Honor system here."

"That leaves me out," Beck says.

"Me, too," I say, shrugging.

"Can I get you something else?"

"Water would be great," I say.

"Coming right up." He turns and crosses the room, grabs a couple bottles from the refrigerator and walks back over to hand one to me.

Holden, Sarah, and Thomas are talking together several yards away. I can feel Holden's gaze on me, but I refuse to look at him.

"So what's your story?" Beck asks.

"Story?"

"Yeah. How'd you get to Nashville?"

"Wing and a prayer?"

He smiles. "How long have you been singing?"

"Longer than I can remember."

"Sounds like it," he says.

Warmth colors my cheeks. I glance down and say, "Thanks. That's nice."

"And true."

"When did you learn to play guitar?"

"When I was still sitting on my daddy's knee. He would hold

me on his lap and put my fingers in position. It's kind of like breathing. Probably like singing for you."

"You're amazing with that guitar," I say and mean it.

"Thanks," he says, and he sounds almost shy. Again, not what I would have expected. "Hey, there's a party down the road some friends of mine are having tonight. You wanna go?"

My immediate inclination is to refuse, but then out of the corner of my eye, I see Sarah lean in and whisper something in Holden's ear and realize what a fool I would be to say no. "Ah, yeah," I say. "That sounds great."

"Cool. Let me see if we're about done here." He walks over to his dad and Rhys, leans down, and they talk for a minute or two.

Case slides his chair back, his long, denim-clad legs stretched out in front of him, his arms folded across his chest. "I think we got some good stuff here tonight, y'all. Rhys, you think you'll have something to listen to maybe tomorrow?"

"Sure," Rhys says. "Late afternoon?"

"All right then, I guess we can call it a night," Case says.

"We really can't thank you enough, man," Holden says. "This has been incredible to say the least."

"Paying it forward and all that." Case says, nodding at Holden. "Have y'all come up with a name yet?"

"Barefoot Outlook," Holden says without hesitating.

That was quick, I think to myself. But I actually really like it.

"Cool," Case says. "I'll touch base with you tomorrow, okay?"

Holden, Thomas, and Sarah gather up their things and walk over to where I'm still standing with Beck.

"Ready?" Thomas asks, looking at me.

"Ah, actually, I'm going to this thing with Beck." I purposely don't look at Holden, but keep my eyes focused on Thomas.

"What thing?" Holden says.

"Party down the road," Beck says. "Y'all oughta come."

"I've got a budding migraine," Sarah says.

"I'm working in the morning," Thomas adds, "but thanks, man."

Holden doesn't say anything. He just looks at me with a question in his eyes that I wonder if anyone else can read.

I glance away and Beck says, "I'll get her home safely."

"All right. Y'all have fun, man," Thomas says, and they leave the room.

"We're going to that party I told you about earlier, Dad," Beck says, taking my arm and leading me to the door.

"Y'all be careful, son," Case says, his deep, rich voice following us from the room.

"We will, Dad," Beck says. He ducks his head back around the corner and adds, "Can I take your car?"

"As long as you and it both come back in one piece."

"Will do."

We walk through the house, down a long hall lined with framed music awards and a glass cabinet full of gold statues.

"Are you amazed by this like every day?" I ask.

Beck laughs. "I probably should be. But you know, he's my dad."

I laugh then, thinking how unbelievable it is that I am actually here in this house, getting ready to go to a party with Beck Phillips, the only son of a country music legend I've had a crush on most of my life. "This is nuts," I say.

"What?"

"Just *this.* Me being here. You. Nuts."

He takes my hand and lets me precede him through the door that leads from the kitchen to the garage.

"We're not seriously taking this, are we?" I ask, spotting the Ferrari.

"You heard him."

"Oh. My. Gosh."

He laughs then, opens the door, and I slide inside, pinching myself just for good measure. Yep, I'm really here.

He goes around to the driver's side, hits the remote to the garage door and backs out. The engine sounds like pure, spun money. That Italian roar that is unique to wealth in its Nth degree.

He guns the car down the driveway, the board fences on either side rolling by in a blur of white. A beep signals the gate and the wrought iron opens at the end of the driveway like Alladin's cave.

Beck swings the car onto the road, and although I glance over to see that we're staying with the speed limit, it feels like we're flying. He lets back the sunroof, and the night air tousles our hair and cools the heat in my cheeks.

"So whose party?" I ask above the wind.

"Macey Canterwood," he answers. "She's kind of getting to be a big deal with Sony."

"Ah," I say. "I heard her new song on the radio yesterday."

"It's pretty cool."

I stop myself from countering with, "It's frigging awesome." Figuring that might come across as gushing, I say nothing.

"Most everyone here tonight will be pretty cool. I won't lie though. Some of the girls can have claws."

"Hm. Anyone in particular I should look out for?"

"I'll let them dig their own hole. Who knows? Maybe everyone will be on good behavior."

If I'm supposed to feel reassured by this, I don't. Butterflies waft up in my stomach and perch in my throat.

My phone vibrates. I pull it from my pocket. It's a text from Holden.

You okay?

Yeah. How's Sarah?

I took Hank Junior out with Patsy.

Thanks. Sorry about the Sarah question.

Is that why you went with him?

What?

To get back at me?

There's nothing to get back at you for. You have a girlfriend. Case closed.

"Everything all right?" Beck asks.

I click off my phone, realizing how rude I'm being. "Yeah," I say. "Sorry. The guys were just letting me know they'd walked my dog for me."

"What kind of dog?"

"Walker Hound."

Beck gives me a long, considering look. "You're not exactly what you first appear to be, are you?"

"What is that?" I ask.

"Like you oughta be on a walkway somewhere. In five inch heels and a mini skirt."

"Is that a compliment?"

"Actually, yeah. But it's kinda killer that you look so girly and yet you've got a hound."

"He's my best buddy."

"Lucky guy."

"The truth is I doubt I'll ever find a guy who gets me the way he does."

Beck downshifts and swings the car onto an asphalt drive. We roar up the hill, the headlights glinting off horses night-grazing a lush pasture.

The house at the top of the driveway is every bit as enormous as the one we just left. The style is different, kind of California contemporary. I would have imagined it looking out of place in this setting. But it doesn't somehow.

Beck pulls the car into a parking spot and cuts the engine. "Let's go have some fun," he says.

We walk into the house with his arm draped loosely around my shoulder. It seems a little weird to me at first because we just met. And, yeah, because he's not Holden.

But once I catch a glimpse of all the hip, young people milling about, relaxing on cushy leather sofas, talking intently by a bar, laughing at someone who's just jumped in the pool, I'm actually glad to have his arm there. It makes me feel like less of an outsider.

He introduces me around. I recognize faces, managing to contain an oh-my-gosh moment when I find myself shaking hands with one of the band members for Keith Urban. Beck throws me a grin as if he's aware of how hard it is for me not to gush.

A very tall, very gorgeous girl walks up to us, leans in and kisses Beck on the cheek. "Hey, gorgeous," she says.

"Hey, Macey," he says.

"I thought you'd decided not to come," she says, her full lips pouting.

"I sat in on a session with my dad tonight. We just finished up a little while ago."

"Cool," she says. "Who for?"

"CeCe here and a band she's singing with. CeCe, this is Macey Canterwood. Macey, CeCe MacKenzie."

"Hey," she says, offering a hand set off with perfectly manicured nails.

"It's very nice to meet you," I say, shaking her hand and noticing her smile feels a little less than genuine. "I really like your music."

"Thanks," she says, her smile now mega bright. "What kind of band are you in?"

"Little country. Little pop," I answer.

"They've got a cool sound," Beck says. I hear an undercurrent between the two and suspect there is more going on here than I first realized.

Macey's smile now appears to have a razor's edge. "Super," she says, and I wonder who the heck says super these days.

Thinking maybe they need a few moments, I excuse myself for the ladies room, winding my way through group after group of ultra-hip looking twenty-something's.

In the bathroom, I check my phone and find the rest of Holden's text message from earlier.

Be careful, okay?

All is well, I type in even as I picture him in bed with Sarah, her arms wrapped around his waist, her legs entwined with his. I touch up my lipstick and do my best to blank my thoughts of the image.

Beck is waiting for me outside the bathroom door. "Wanna dance?" he asks.

The music has changed from laid back and conversational to upbeat and thumping. I take his hand and follow him outside where people are dancing alongside the pool. He loops an arm around my waist and hooks me up close.

"Those aren't Nashville moves," I say. "More like South Beach."

He grins and says, "I like all kinds of music."

"Me, too, actually."

"I like your moves," he says, ducking his head near my ear.

I smile up at him, wondering if I'm ready to open this door. Is it even fair to him? My heart is tied up in knots over Holden, and yet I know that's a dead end road. Here I am at a hot party in Nashville, dancing with a hot guy. What is there to think about?

The music goes slow, and he swoops me in even closer. His body is fit and hard, but the first thing I register is the differences between him and Holden. Holden is broader, and I can't shake the memory of how we felt together.

I squeeze my eyes shut, wanting so very much to be here, in this moment.

"What are you thinking?" Beck says, tipping my chin up so that I am forced to look into his eyes.

"Nothing," I say, forcing a smile.

"It's that guy, isn't it?"

"Who?"

"Holden."

"Has a girlfriend."

"Does your heart know that?"

"Yes. It does," I say, my tone conceding even as I try to sound indifferent.

"I've kinda been there," Beck says, trailing his thumb across my jawline. "I know what it feels like."

I tip my head back a little farther and let a little of my pain show on my face.

"When something doesn't work, you have to move on. I'd be more than happy to help you with that." He leans in and butterfly kisses me. "I'd really like to help you with that."

"Mind if I have a turn?"

Macey Canterwood has her hand on my shoulder, the smile on her face suggesting she has no intention of taking no for an answer.

"We're kind of in the middle of something, Mace," Beck says.

"I can see that," she says, "but I have something to share with you. Just one song."

"It's fine," I say, backing away. "I'll go catch my breath."

"He's quite the dancer, isn't he?" Macey says, her smile now nowhere near reaching her eyes.

"Don't go far," Beck tells me. "This won't take long."

I make my way back inside the party, stand in line for the restroom and then use the ninety seconds before someone starts knocking to run a brush through my hair and touch up my long-gone lipstick.

Back at the bar, I ask for a bottle of water, but just as the nose-ringed bartender starts to hand it to me, a voice behind me says, "Hold off on that! Girl, if you're planning to hang with the likes of Beck Phillips, you gotta learn how to party at least a little."

I turn to find Macey smiling at me. She shakes a finger at the bartender and says, "We'll have two of what you made me earlier."

The bartender looks at Macey and raises an eyebrow, which also happens to have a ring in it. "New friend?" he asks.

"Yes," Macey answers. "CeCe, meet Huxton. Huxton, CeCe."

"Hey," he says. "Any friend of Macey's–"

"Nice to meet you," I say. "I'm fine with the water. I should go find Beck."

"He asked me to tell you he's grabbing a game of ping pong downstairs. Why don't *we* grab a chat and get to know each other a bit?"

You know that little voice that dings inside you when something isn't quite right, but you can't pinpoint it closely enough to act on it? I'm hearing the ding, but she *is* Macey Canterwood. Her music is being played all over the radio, and what do I have to lose by trying to leave here tonight with her as something closer to a friend than an enemy?

"Go snag that sofa for us," Macey says. "I'll get our drinks."

I push away from the bar and do exactly that, even as I ask myself what the two of us could possibly have in common. Except Beck, of course. And the fact that she obviously wants him, and sees me as a threat.

The couch is cushy and comfortable. I sink onto it with a sudden awareness of fatigue and exactly how long this day has been. What I really want is to go home and curl up in bed with Hank Junior.

Macey strides over in her four-inch heels – she must wear them all the time to be that competent in them – and hands me a glass that at least looks appealing. "A little something I like before a show – nothing crazy – just knocks the edge off."

"What's in it?"

"Pineapple and Goji berry juice. Which is really good for you, by the way. I'll let you guess the rest."

I've never been one to feel peer pressure. It's not something I ever bought into in high school. I had my thing – music – other kids had their thing. I didn't yearn to be someone that I wasn't.

But here, in this place, in Nashville, I realize just how far at the bottom of the totem pole I am. How high the climb is. And when someone from way on up the ladder, reaches down and offers you a hand past some of those rungs, it's pretty tempting to take it.

I sip the drink tentatively, expecting somehow that it will taste gosh-awful. Only it doesn't. "Um, good," I say.

"Told you you'd like it," she says, turning up her own glass and then stretching back on the couch. She crosses her incredibly long legs in front of her. Next to her, I definitely feel like the country mouse. "What are your goals, CeCe?"

"To sing," I answer.

She laughs. "But where?"

"Wherever anyone will listen, I guess," I answer simply but truthfully.

"I remember that feeling," she says. "But you probably shouldn't say it out loud. It has a hint of desperation to it."

"But aren't you here because you love to sing?" I ask her.

"Yes. But other things go with it that I also love."

"Such as?"

"Recognition. Adoration." She laughs. "I get how that sounds. But if you're here, trying to make it in this business, you like those things, too. Maybe you're not willing to admit it yet, but you do."

I take another sip of my drink and wonder if it's true. "I've never thought about that part of it."

"We're all a little narcissistic at heart. At least when we get the chance to be. Don't you think we're always looking for that chance?"

The edges of my vision start to fuzz, and I blink to clear it away. "I like to think I'm looking for the chance to do what I love to do."

"At the risk of someone else getting to do what they love to do though, right?"

I'm not sure how I've waded into this conversation, but it's starting to feel like quicksand, and I'd like to back out. Only my legs feel heavy and weighted, or is that my thoughts? "I don't know. I don't feel exactly–"

"What's wrong?" Macey asks, her voice sounding like it's coming to me remixed with heavy bass.

I try to stand. My legs feel as though the bones have been removed, and they won't hold me upright. I drop back onto the couch, grabbing a cushion to right myself.

Macey stands, staring down at me from what seems like a thousand feet up. I can barely hear her voice when she says, "Good luck with your ambitions, CeCe. Just don't let them get in the way of common sense, okay?"

She turns and walks away. I raise a hand to stop her, to ask her to get Beck. Only I realize I can't make the words come out. I slump back against the sofa, trying to hold my eyelids open. They're so heavy, weighted with stone. Maybe I can let them close for just a minute. Just long enough for me to work up enough energy to fight back to the surface.

But it feels so good to give in. Float along with the current carrying me away. Warm sun. Ocean breeze. Oblivion.

♪

Holden

I can't sleep.

I try, staying to my side of the bed, Sarah to hers. She's been asleep for a while as far as I can tell, but I don't think either of us wants to talk to each other, so she could be pretending, I guess.

I look at the clock. 1:15.

CeCe's not home yet. I've been listening for the door, and if I'm honest with myself, that's why I'm still awake.

I can't quit thinking about her with him. Can't quit wondering what they're doing. If he's tried to kiss her yet. If she's let him.

That last thought catapults me out of bed. I grab a t-shirt, shrug into it and leave the room. Patsy and Hank Junior are hunkered together on the sofa. They raise their heads and look at me with sleepy eyes. "Anyone up for a walk?" I ask.

Patsy ducks her head behind the pillow, giving me her answer. Hank Junior hops down and trots over.

I pick up his leash, grab my keys and cell phone from the table by the door, and we head outside. The night air is cool. At the bottom of the stairs, I hook on his leash. We walk fast down the sidewalk, and when Hank Junior clearly wants to go faster, I decide to run.

Hank's couch potato lounging could fool you about his athletic ability. The dog can run. He's made for it, and he loves it. I love it, too. We let it rip for a couple of blocks, Hank sprinting in pure joy, me trying to drain the battery of my imagination.

And it works, until we both start to tire. We drop to a jog for several blocks, and then a walk during which Hank is intent on letting others know we were here.

I'm breathing hard and heavy, but I'm right back to thinking about CeCe, wondering why she's not home yet.

"Should I call her, Hank?"

He turns to look at me with a raised ear and wags his tail.

"That a yes?"

He barks once.

"All right, then."

I tap her name under recent calls and wait while it rings. Twice. Three times. Four. Voice mail picks up.

"No answer," I direct to Hank. He looks up at me and whines.

"Yeah, me, too," I say. We turn around at the end of the block and start walking back.

It's not my place to worry about CeCe, but I am worried. About her safety or what she might be doing with Beck? Both, I guess.

Everything about what I'm feeling is so messed up. She has every right to be out with Beck Phillips or whoever else she wants to be out with. I'm the one without that right.

We're just short of the apartment building when a black Ferrari turns into the parking lot. I recognize it as belonging to Case Phillips and assume Beck drove it tonight.

The car pulls in front of the building, and the engine goes silent. I stop before they spot me, wondering if I'm going to have to wait here in the shadows while Beck Phillips makes out with CeCe.

The driver's side door opens with a *wachunk*. Beck slides out and jogs around to the passenger door. He opens it, then disappears from sight. I see him squat down, wait for him to stand back up. A minute. Two. Four. Okay, seems weird.

Deciding I'm not waiting any longer, I lead Hank through the parking lot and past the car. He turns around and barks, then starts tugging at the lead.

Beck stands and calls out, "Hey, man."

His voice doesn't sound quite right. I turn, glimpse the concern on his face.

"Hey," I say. "What's up?"

"CeCe's kind of out of it," he says, raking a hand through his hair.

I jog over behind a still tugging Hank Junior who wedges in between Beck and the car to plant two paws on the seat and begin licking CeCe's cheek.

I look past Beck to see CeCe out cold, not responding at all to Hank's licking. "What the—" I start, shoving Beck around to look at me. "What did you do to her?"

Beck holds up two hands, backing away. "Hold on, man. It wasn't me."

"Wasn't you what?" I hear my voice rising and force myself not to go ahead and punch his country-music-star-rich-kid-ass all the way back to his daddy's estate.

"A girl at the party put something in her drink to make her sleep."

"Why?" I ask, biting out the word.

"We used to date," he says, to his credit, sounding miserably sorry. "I never should have left CeCe alone with her."

"What did she give her?"

"Sleeping pill."

"Are you sure?"

"Yeah."

"How?"

"Because I told her I'd tell my dad what she'd done if she didn't tell me, and I would ask him to tell everybody he knows in the music business."

I believe him. I can see he's telling the truth, and that he feels guilty as all get out.

"Let's get her upstairs," I say.

"Yeah," Beck agrees.

We both lean in at the same time to lift her out and knock foreheads.

"Crap!"

"Ow!"

We jump back, glaring at one another while Hank Junior looks up at us like we're the two biggest dufusses he's ever had the misfortune to run across. And he might be right.

"I'll get her," I say.

Beck stands back, two hands in the air, as if in concession to the fact that I have some unspoken right to being in charge from here on out. I'm not about to tell him I don't.

I swing CeCe up in my arms and head for the stairs, Hank Junior at my heels. I hear the car door thunk closed, look over my shoulder to see Beck striding after me. "You should go home," I say.

"I'm not leaving until I know she's okay," he shoots back, and I can hear him digging in his heels.

I decide at that point to ignore him and head up the stairway with CeCe tight against my chest. I dig my key out of my pocket and decide to make use of Tag-Along, after all. I hand it to him, then barely wait for him to get the door open, before pushing past him into the living room.

I lower CeCe onto the sofa, propping her head up with a pillow. I sit down beside her then, rubbing my thumb across her jawline. "Hey, CeCe, wake up. CeCe?"

"I'll get a glass of water," Beck says, heading for the kitchen.

Hank Junior jumps up on the couch and starts licking CeCe's face.

Realizing he has a better chance at being Prince Charming than I do, I don't ask him to stop.

She moans a little, and I feel a ping of relief at the sound. She flops the back of her hand across her face in response to Hank's kissing. He wags his tail and licks harder.

But she's not responding now, and I get that sick feeling of worry in my stomach again.

Beck returns with the water, and he holds the back of her head up while I try to get her to take a sip. But she won't, and it trails down the side of her face instead.

"We could put her in the shower," Beck says.

I glance up at him with enough dagger to make him take a step back.

"With her clothes on, of course," Beck says quickly.

"I assumed as much," I say, giving him a square look.

I pick her up from the couch and carry her down the hall to her room. As soon as I open the door, the scent of her perfume meets my nose, sending a curl of memory up from somewhere inside me. And then I'm thinking about the last time I smelled this scent on her neck and how I would forever associate it with the taste of her kiss.

Hank Junior follows us into the room and hops up on the bed to survey our intentions, I would guess. I leave the bathroom door open and ease her onto the shower floor.

Beck tests the water and makes sure it's warm enough before turning on the spray. We point the nozzle at the top of her head and wait for it to work. It takes a surprisingly long time. Maybe it's seconds, but it seems like minutes. Several. I'm holding my breath, and only realize it when she begins to shake her head, batting a hand at the spray.

She moans and says, "Stop. What is that–"

"CeCe," I say. "It's me. Holden. You're back at the apartment. In the shower. We're trying to wake you up. You've kind of been out of it."

"What happened?" she asks, her voice groggy and a little slurred.

"Someone spiked your drink," Beck says, stepping into view.

She looks up, her eyelids so heavy she can barely hold them open. "Who would do that?"

I turn to look at Beck, admittedly feeling a little pleased with the guilt he feels.

"Maybe we should talk about it when you're feeling better," he says.

"Are you all right, CeCe?" I ask. "I can take you to the ER and get you checked out if you want."

"No, no," she says. "I'm okay. I'm just. . .really sleepy."

"What's going on in here?"

I turn to find Thomas standing in the doorway, wearing a pair of polka dot boxers and running his hand through sleep-wild hair.

I raise an eyebrow and drop a look at the boxers. "Seriously?"

"Gift from Mama," he says, sheepish.

"Scary," I say.

Thomas peers around me. "What the heck happened to CeCe?"

Beck hangs his head and says. "Victim of one of my messed up friends."

"You all right, CeCe?" Thomas asks.

"Yeah. Can I just go to bed?" she says. "Alone."

The three of us guys look at each other, and take a step back.

"Sure," I say. "If you need some help getting–"

"I don't. I'm all good. Really."

"All right if I call you in the morning?" Beck throws out behind me. "I have some serious apologizing to do."

"She's working tomorrow. Today." Whatever. Anything to get him to leave.

"Can I drive you?" he asks, peering over my shoulder and trying to make eye contact with CeCe.

Sarah appears in the doorway then. She's wearing a strappy pink nightgown, and her hair is tousled from sleep. "What's going on in here?"

CeCe looks at her and then glances back at me. "Nothing," she says. "Everybody go back to bed."

She starts to get up, falters a little, and grabs on to the side of the shower.

"Here," I say, reaching out a hand to steady her.

But she avoids my touch and says, "Please. Can everyone just leave?"

We back out of the bathroom, Sarah asking, "What happened to her?"

Thomas takes Sarah's arm and says, "Come on. Let's go."

They leave the room. CeCe reaches for a robe on the back of the door, pressing it to her chest, and without either looking at Beck or me, says, "Goodnight."

"Are you sure you're all right?" I start.

"Yes. Please. Go."

"I'm really sorry, CeCe," Beck says. "I'll check on you in the morning."

"Thanks," she says.

He turns and walks out of the room then.

Once he's gone, I look at CeCe and say, "I can stay. Just to make sure—"

"I don't want you to," she says. "Sarah's waiting for you. In your room. Go."

I hear the frustration in her voice. "What happened tonight, CeCe?" I ask.

"A jealous girl. That's all that happened."

"She drugged you. That's all that happened?"

"I'm fine," she says. "I just want to go to bed."

"CeCe. We need to talk."

"No. We don't. We really don't. There's nothing to talk about."

"But I want to explain something."

She bites her lip and looks at me with eyes on the verge of tears.

"He's not a guy you should be hanging out with, CeCe."

Her eyes go wide, and she laughs abruptly. "And you are? You have a girlfriend, Holden. A serious girlfriend. One who drove all the way from Atlanta to be here with you. A girlfriend who seems to want to move here to be with you. What in that equation allows anything at all for you and me?"

I want to tell her that none of that is true. Only it is. "CeCe."

"What?" she asks. "Can you deny any of that?"

"No," I say.

"Then why are you not in there with her where you belong?"

I look at her for several long drawn out moments. I think about all the things I could say. All the things I should say. But I don't want to say any of them. I just want to say the truth. "Because I want to be in here with you."

She presses her lips together, and again, I see how close she is to tears. "You don't have that right," she says.

I want to deny it, to argue with her, to bring up all the ifs, and the buts, and the maybes, but she's right. All I can say that is absolutely true is that I want her.

"Holden, I'm wet. I'm cold. I'm tired. Please."

I try to stop myself from asking this question, but I can't. The words come rolling out. "Did you go with him tonight because of me?"

Her eyes widen a little, and I can see her considering the answer. "Do you mean did I go to make you jealous?"

I shrug. I somehow know what she's going to say. And how arrogant is it of me anyway to think that would be the reason she went.

She folds her arms across her chest and sets her gaze somewhere just to the right of mine. "No," she says. "He's a nice guy. I went because I wanted to go."

Her words slam into me like baseballs being hurled from a major league pitcher. I guess I didn't want to believe that was true, but how stupid could I be? He's Beck Phillips. His father's a major country music star. What girl wouldn't want to go out with him? "Okay," I say, backing out of the room. "Goodnight, CeCe."

"Goodnight," she says.

And I don't let myself look back. Only a fool would look back.

♪

CeCe

I've never been a good liar.

But my lie is the first thing I think about when I wake up at just after ten. That and the look on Holden's face.

Considering how I've had to watch him with Sarah and act as if it doesn't bother me a single iota – the way she holds onto him, the way she looks at him as if there's no question that he is hers.

But then doesn't she have that right?

Hank snuggles up against me, and I know I need to get up and take him out. My head throbs dully. I feel like I haven't had a glass of water in two years.

Did I go with Beck last night to make Holden jealous? The question pops up like a red flag.

Not entirely.

But somewhat?

Maybe.

I throw on some running clothes, grab Hank's leash and slip out of the apartment without seeing anyone.

I know Thomas had to work this morning, but the last thing I want to think about is whether Holden and Sarah are sleeping in and what they might be doing if they are.

Since I'm already in my running clothes, I decide to pound some of last night's toxins out of me and take off at a good pace. Hank Junior is always up for a run of any kind and needs no encouragement.

We go out about two miles and I turn back. A half-mile or so from the apartment, we walk. A car pulls up alongside us, beeping its horn. I glance over and spot Beck in a convertible BMW, an uncertain look on his face.

"Hey," he says.

"Hey," I say.

"You're doing pretty well to already have a run under your belt."

"Figured my body could use it," I say.

"Yeah, about that—"

"Let's not," I say. "Better to leave it alone."

"Buy you a coffee."

"You don't have to do that."

"What if I said I want to?"

"I've got Hank."

"He'll fit nicely in the back seat."

"He's not used to rides this nice."

"It's a car. Four wheels. Come on."

"I could use the coffee. That much is true," I say.

He reaches over to open the passenger door for me. Hank hops over the seat and into the back, sitting straight as if he's prepared to enjoy the view.

Starbucks is packed with Vanderbilt students, sitting at the outside tables with laptops poised in front of them.

"Drive through okay?" Beck asks.

"Sure."

He asks me what I'd like, and I tell him a tall Veranda with one sugar. He goes for a black Pikes Peak. The girl at the drive-through window smiles big at him and asks if it's okay if Hank has a treat. I nod, and she hands Beck a cookie.

He holds it back for Hank to take, and he sits munching in happiness.

We sip our coffee in silence as we pull away from the Starbucks. We're a few blocks from the apartment when he says, "I didn't sleep last night, thinking about what could have happened."

"It wasn't your fault."

"Actually, I should have known better than to leave you with her."

"You didn't. Look, everything worked out all right. I won't be buying her latest single though."

Beck laughs. "Me, either. You could press charges against her or something if you wanted to."

"I don't want to. I just want to forget it. Maybe take it as a lesson learned about being a naïve, gullible–"

"Hey," he says. "You're not gullible. She's just bad."

We pull into the parking lot of the apartment building. Beck cuts the engine. He angles toward me in his seat and says, "I'd really like to make it up to you."

"That's not necessary."

"Please. Let me."

I sigh, reach back to rub Hank Junior under his chin. "So what do you have in mind?"

"Dad's writing with Bobby Jenkins later this afternoon. He's one of the top writers in town."

"I know who he is. That's great."

"I'm going with him. I thought maybe you'd like to come, too."

"Sit in on a session with Bobby Jenkins?"

"Yeah. He's a cool guy. He writes amazing songs."

"Wow. You don't have to do this."

"I know. I want to."

"I'm supposed to work tonight."

"Maybe you could get someone to take your shift."

"Maybe," I say. "I'll try. Give me your number, and I'll call you in a bit to let you know if I can get off."

He tells me the number, and I punch it into my phone. "Send me yours?"

"Sure."

"Thanks for the coffee." I get out of the car, motion for Hank Junior to follow me and then shut the door, stepping onto the curb.

Footsteps sound on the stairway behind us. I glance over my shoulder to spot Holden and Sarah walking toward us. Sarah has her hand tucked inside his arm. He spots us, and maybe it's only me who notices the way his eyes go a deeper blue.

"Hey," Beck says.

"Y'all are out early," Sarah says.

"Figured I owed her a coffee at the very least," Beck says.

"Yeah, I've yet to hear the real story of what happened last night," she says, looking at me with raised eyebrows. "That must have been some party."

"A little more than we bargained for," Beck replies.

"Had to have been fun if you two are already at it again," Sarah adds.

Holden is yet to speak, and the response on the tip of my tongue isn't one that would make Sarah and me friends. "Thanks again, Beck," I say.

"See you later this afternoon."

"I'll try."

"You better," he adds.

Hank and I cross the parking lot and make for the stairwell. I can feel Holden's eyes on us, but I just keep walking.

♪

AS IT TURNS OUT, I am able to switch shifts with Ainsley, one of the other waitresses at the restaurant. She's glad to do it, she says, since I offer to take her shift tomorrow night and there was something she wanted to do anyway.

I text Beck and let him know.

I feed Hank Junior early and leave Holden a note that I've fed Patsy, too.

My clothes selection isn't vast, so it doesn't take me long to decide on a simple pink sundress and flat sandals.

Beck is driving the BMW again, top down, and it feels good sliding down the Nashville streets with music from his iPhone blasting through the car's speakers.

"You look great," he says, glancing over at me, smiling his confident smile, one hand on the steering wheel.

"Thank you," I say, and feel myself blush a little.

Being with Beck feels different from being with Holden. With Holden, I always feel on the edge of something about to happen. Something I very much want but am also very much afraid of.

Not that I couldn't be intimidated by Beck. He's lived a life I know very little about. A life I have dreamed about but don't know in reality.

And he's gorgeous. Who wouldn't be intimidated by that? But he's also young. My age. And that makes him easier to talk to. Easier to be with in some ways. And then again, there's that small difference of him not having a girlfriend looming in between us.

"So the studio where we're going," Beck says, "is really cool. Bobby can pretty much write with whoever he wants considering his track record. And it's deserved. At least that's what my dad says."

"I think I know every song he's ever written," I say. "Are you sure it's okay if I'm here?"

"Positive. I checked with my dad."

It takes us twenty minutes or so to get there, the house not as far outside the city as Beck's house. When we pull into the driveway, I spot the Ferrari, indicating that Case must already be here.

Beck pulls up beside it, gets out and comes around to open my door.

"Thanks," I say, sliding out and trying to subdue the sudden flutter of butterflies in my stomach. "I'm nervous."

"Don't be. Everything's really laid back here."

The house isn't nearly as grand as Case's, but impressive all the same. It's a classic brick style with an antiqued wood front door and a mammoth knocker shaped like a guitar.

Beck knocks and a few seconds later, a pretty woman somewhere in her forties answers the door. Her smile is welcoming and we follow her through the house to a studio set up very much like the one at Beck's house. It's not as big though, and the equipment seems a little less fancy, more like the workhorse version.

Case and the man I instantly recognize as Bobby Jenkins are sitting together at a round table. I saw him once in an interview on the country music channel. Both men have guitars on their laps. Beck introduces me.

"It's really nice to meet you, Mr. Jenkins." He's older than I expect, maybe late fifties.

"So glad you could be here."

"Thank you so much. Really."

Case told him about the recording session yesterday and how I'm part of a group called Barefoot Outlook. It sounds strange hearing it as if it's really happening, and while I'd like to believe it's true, it feels more like something made of toothpicks than beams.

"Well, good luck to you," he says.

"You got anything you want to start with, Case?" he asks, picking up the guitar.

"Just a phrase," Case says. "Don't have too much attached to it yet."

"What is it?"

"Wishing time away."

Bobby nods. "Hmm. Yeah. See what we can do with that." He throws out some angles, some kind of obvious, some not so much.

I listen to the rally between them, mesmerized at the process and can't help but think how much Holden would love this. The two of them are like miners, digging, sifting, rinsing, until they find the lines of gold nuggets that begin to form a verse, a chorus, a bridge. The pieces put together with such expertise that I can't really imagine ever reaching this level of capability.

The music they create fits the words perfectly, like a glove to a fine-boned hand.

Three hours have passed when they push back their chairs and smile at each other.

"Yeah," Case says. "I like it."

"Me, too," Bobby agrees.

Beck and I glance at each other and smile. Neither of us has said a word since the start of the session, and I wonder how many times he has seen this done.

They call it a wrap. We stand, and Case throws an arm around Beck's shoulders, giving him a hug.

Beck shakes hands with Bobby who looks at me and says, "Really glad you could be here."

"Thank you," I say. "So much. It was a priceless experience."

He smiles at me and nods. When he doesn't poo poo my extravagant praise, I wonder if someone had once done the same for him, someone who was really great at writing the same as he was.

We're in the car on the way back into town when I say, "That was really incredible, Beck. I don't know how to thank you."

"I think I owed you one," he says. "It was cool for me, too. I haven't gotten over being amazed by the whole process yet. It's kind of like magic or something."

I know what he means. It is like that, watching something amazing being conjured out of thin air, the pieces coming together to form something beautiful and possibly able to resonate with so many people.

"It's early. You wanna go somewhere and hang out a while? There's a good band over at Lauren's place."

"Can we have an honest moment?"

"Sure," he says.

"I like you, Beck. I really like you. Who wouldn't? But my head is kind of somewhere else right now."

"Holden," he says.

"It's not something I won't get past. I really don't have a choice. So maybe if you could just give me a little time?"

"That's more than cool," he says. "Let's just hang out. No expectations. No demands. How's that sound?"

"I don't know. Like maybe you're too good to be true?"

He laughs. "Or maybe I just know a good thing when I see it, and I don't want to blow it." He reaches out and brushes my cheek with the back of his hand. "Let's just go have some fun, okay?"

"Okay," I say. And that sounds like a great idea to me.

♪

THE RESTAURANT IS CRAZY busy. There's a line flowing out the main door and down the sidewalk several storefronts long.

Beck knows the guy behind the rope and gets waved in, towing me along behind him.

"I feel really funny about that," I say as we slip inside the low-lit interior.

"Funny enough to go stand at the end of that line?"

"Um. Maybe not?"

The band playing on stage is country with a thumping beat, and you can't help but instantly feel it in your bones and want to move to it.

Holden isn't supposed to be working tonight, so I start at the sight of him behind the bar, filling glasses with ice. As if he feels my gaze on him, he looks up and suddenly we're staring straight at one another, my heart kicking up instantly.

In that moment of blank honesty, I see the flash of hurt in his eyes.

There's no justification for it. He has no say over who I'm here with, but at the same time, I know that feeling. It's the same one I get when I see him with Sarah, and I realize that it gives me no pleasure to make him feel that.

He turns his back and smiles at a woman at the bar. I watch its effect on her, the way she leans in and stares up at him. I turn away abruptly as my stomach does a somersault of hurt, unreasonable as it is.

As it turns out, Beck knows a couple of the band members, and we snag a table up close. During the first set, I sit as if anchored to my seat, focusing on absorbing every note of every song. The lead singer is incredible. She's got a voice that flows from her like warm honey and a range that makes me instantly envious. She also has the kind of looks that make listening to her nearly secondary to watching her.

They take a break after the first set and the singer comes over to our table.

"Hey, Beck," she says. "Glad y'all could come out."

"Hey, Tania. You're rockin' it tonight."

"Thanks," she says with an appreciative smile.

"Tania, this is CeCe MacKenzie."

"Y'all are great," I say. "I love your sound."

"Thanks," she says, turning her smile to me. "We've been working hard at it."

"No doubt," Beck says. "Y'all are really getting the polish on it."

"Thank you." She looks at Beck, her eyes suddenly teasing. "Is she why you never called me back?"

Most guys would have been embarrassed by that kind of direct arrow, but Beck shrugs and says, "Nooo. But she could be."

Tania laughs. "Don't worry. I'm on to greener pastures."

And for some reason, what's between them doesn't feel like anything other than good-natured ribbing. No daggers like there had been with Macey last night.

The rest of the show is great, and Beck seems to know half the people in the place, but I'm relieved when the band plays its last encore, and we head out into the night.

I manage to leave without meeting eyes with Holden again. "That was awesome," I say as we get in the car. "Thank you for asking me."

"Yeah, they're pretty cool." Beck cranks the music, and we speed down the highway. We both seem content not to talk, and when we get back to the apartment, he cuts the engine, insisting on walking me to the door.

"That was really fun," I say, sticking my key in the lock and turning to look up at him.

"Thanks for going with me."

"Thanks for asking."

"So we're stuck on that friends thing, huh?" he says, a smile touching the corner of his mouth.

"For now?"

"For now. I think you're worth it," he says. "The wait, I mean."

Footsteps sound on the stairwell, and I look over Beck's shoulder to see Holden come to an abrupt stop at the sight of us.

"Sorry," he says, and I can see he's caught off guard. "Excuse me." He cuts around us, pulling my key out of the lock and handing it to me. He inserts his own and opens the door. He goes inside without saying another word.

The awkwardness left in his wake is thick and undeniable.

"A little time?" I say.

"A little time," he agrees. "Goodnight, CeCe. Sleep well, okay?"

"You, too." And with that, I watch him walk away.

♪

Holden

I absolutely HATE this feeling.

Jealous guys suck. I mean, what is jealousy anyway?

Awareness that there's something you can't have. Or that someone is better at something than you are. Or has someone you can't have.

There it is. Large and looming. The truth. Ugly as it is.

Someone I can't have.

I grab a beer from the refrigerator, pull out a drawer for the opener, pop it off and take a long drink. I head for the shower then just because I don't want to be standing here when CeCe comes in.

The water is cold but does pretty much nothing to cool my misery. In my room, I wait until I hear her door click closed, and then I step out into the hall and knock.

She doesn't respond for several moments, which tells me she's considering not answering. "CeCe?" I say.

The door opens and she stands there looking at me with What? on her face.

"Ainsley asked me to remind you about her shift tomorrow."

"I know."

"Okay." Awkward silence, and then I manage, "How was it?"

"It was great. All of it. Great." She's quiet for a moment and then, "Where's Sarah?"

I glance away and then back at her. "She went back to Georgia. We kind of had a fight."

CeCe steps away, and I can see her blank her expression. "Oh. I'm sorry."

"Are you?" I ask.

"Yes, I am."

"Why?"

She throws up her hands. "Why wouldn't I be? You're obviously crazy about each other and–"

"Are we?" It's a question I shouldn't ask, but I can't help myself.

"Yes! You are!"

"Don't you want to know what we fought about?"

"No, I don't think I do."

"You," he says. "We fought about you."

She blinks once. Hard. And then, "Why would you be fighting about me?"

"Because she knows."

"There's nothing to know."

"Knows it's different. Since I got here. Since. . .since I met you."

"Holden. Don't do this. Don't hang this on me. I don't want to be responsible for you breaking Sarah's heart."

"I'm not hanging anything on you. I'm just telling you the truth."

"You love her."

"I did. Yes, I did. Now, I don't know anymore."

"She loves you," CeCe says.

"She says she does. I'm not sure what that means based on the way we've been to each other since she got here. And I wonder now if we've just been trying to make each other fit what it is we both say we want. People change, don't they? And when the change comes, how long do you deny it?"

"Holden–"

Her protest is weaker than before, and as if the words are pulled from me, I say, "I can't stand seeing you with him."

"We're friends, Holden."

"He doesn't want to be friends with you, CeCe."

"I've told him that right now that's all we can be."

"Why?"

She drops her gaze. "Because I'm not ready."

"Because," I interrupt. "You think about me the way I think about you. With every breath. Every thought."

"No, I don't. I–"

I reach out and loop my arm around her waist, splay my hand across the dip of her lower back. I reel her to me, slowly, steadily, as if the catch is inevitable. She bumps to a stop against my chest, tips her head back and looks up at me.

"Holden, don't. This is not where we should go."

"There's nowhere else I want to go," I say. "In fact, if we don't go there, if we don't go there now–" I swoop in then, finding her mouth with mine. The kiss is deep and so full of longing and want that I instantly feel inebriated by it. My head is buzzing, like I just took a shot of some fine tequila. But this buzz is better. So much better.

I lift her to me, my hands at her waist. She wraps her arms around my neck and kisses me back, fully, giving in, no longer protesting or coming up with reasons why I shouldn't be here.

We just kiss. And I feel like we could kiss like this all night long, and I wouldn't be able to get enough of her.

I pick her up, lifting and carrying her all at the same time to the bed. I both drop her and follow her down at the same time. The feel of her beneath me is like being found when I never knew I was lost.

Hank Junior makes a sound that might be disapproval and heads to a corner of the room.

CeCe and I roll to the middle, still kissing. It's pretty clear that neither of us has any desire to stop.

I feel something crumple under me and pull a piece of paper out from under my shoulder.

I'm ready to toss it when CeCe grabs my hand and says, "Hank Junior! What have you gotten into now?"

The edges of the paper have been chewed, the top right hand corner completely missing. CeCe glances at it, then pulls it in for a closer look.

Her face goes completely still. She slides up on her knees, her face growing whiter as she reads.

"What is it?" I raise up on my elbow. "What's wrong?"

She drops the paper, and it flutters back onto the blanket beneath us.

The look on her face has me spooked, and I cautiously pick up the torn page and start to read.

Patient Sarah Saxon
Age: 22
Female
Recommended course of treatment:
Radiation, chemotherapy. Initial course to be followed by reevaluation for surgical candidacy.

I sit up and swing my legs over the side of the bed, elbows on my knees, feeling suddenly and completely sick.

I hold the paper under the lamplight and read it again, just to make sure I hadn't imagined it.

"Holden," CeCe says, putting a hand on my back.

"That's why she came," I say. "To tell me. She came here to tell me. I didn't–"

"You didn't know. You didn't know."

"I all but pushed her out the door. Oh, my God." I really think I am going to be sick. I lean over and cross my arms over my stomach. I can feel the blood pounding in my temples.

CeCe gets up, stands in front of me and drops to her knees, forcing me to look at her. "You haven't done anything wrong," she says. "You haven't."

I look up at her, and it feels like I'm on one of those crazy amusement park rides that zooms you to a peak and then lets you plummet. This is the plummet part. "How can you say that?"

"Because it's true," she says, her voice breaking in the middle of the statement. "She needs you."

I let myself look directly at her then, at the tears suddenly coursing down her face. I realize they are for Sarah. For us. For it all.

♪

Next: Book Three – What We Feel

About Inglath Cooper

RITA® Award-winning author Inglath Cooper was born in Virginia. She is a graduate of Virginia Tech with a degree in English. She fell in love with books as soon as she learned how to read. "My mom read to us before bed, and I think that's how I started to love stories. It was like a little mini-vacation we looked forward to every night before going to sleep. I think I eventually read most of the books in my elementary school library."

That love for books translated into a natural love for writing and a desire to create stories that other readers could get lost in, just as she had gotten lost in her favorite books. Her stories focus on the dynamics of relationships, those between a man and a woman, mother and daughter, sisters, friends. They most often take place in small Virginia towns very much like the one where she grew up and are peopled with characters who reflect those values and traditions.

"There's something about small-town life that's just part of who I am. I've had the desire to live in other places, wondered what it would be like to be a true Manhattanite, but the thing I know I would miss is the familiarity of faces everywhere I go. There's a lot to be said for going in the grocery store and seeing ten people you know!"

Inglath Cooper is an avid supporter of companion animal rescue and is a volunteer and donor for the Franklin County Humane Society. She and her family have fostered many dogs and cats that have gone on to be adopted by other families. "The rewards are endless. It's an eye-opening moment to realize that what one person throws away can fill another person's life with love and joy."

Follow Inglath on Facebook
at www.facebook.com/inglathcooperbooks

Join her mailing list for news of new releases and giveaways at www.inglathcooper.com

Made in the USA
Monee, IL
28 May 2020